DEATH IN PARADISE

HAWAII THRILLER SERIES

J.E. TRENT

For my wife Eila, who was a continuous source of encouragement to write this story. I'm eternally grateful.

BONUS

Get the free prequel and new release notifications.
https://readerlinks.com/1/965413

1

MORNING PADDLE

Kona Hawaii

There's nothing like a hot-blooded Filipina with a bad attitude pointing a butterfly knife at you first thing in the morning to get your adrenaline pumping. That wasn't Mike Murphy's preferred way to start the day. Once again, Simmy had accused him of cheating on her with another woman. And he was sick of it. It was 6:30 a.m. as the sun rose over Hualalai Mountain and turned the puffy white clouds above Kailua Bay cotton candy pink.

Mike paddled his one-man canoe over the reef, heading toward Kaiwi Point. Most days he paddled south toward Keauhou. But that morning there was a fishing tournament about to start in Kona. There were twenty-five boats entered, they jockeyed for the best position near the Kailua Pier, and he didn't want to get tangled up with them.

Those rich guys were trying to get the jump on the other boats at the start of the tournament. They could be cutthroat as they raced off to the fishing grounds. A canoe, versus a forty-five-foot Cabo fishing yacht, doesn't get any right-of-way. But what the canoe might get was flipped by the wake.

And it was too early in the morning to huli the boat as far as he was concerned.

Mike used his time on the ocean every morning to think about life in general and whatever he had planned for the day. Today, he had two pressing issues. One of them was a woman who loved him in an unhealthy jealous kind of way. And the other, a billionaire neighbor who wanted to buy his small resort, Aloha Village, so it could be bulldozed and replaced with a casino mega-resort.

Mike tried to quit thinking about his crazy girlfriend and just be at one with the ocean while he dug his paddle deep into the water with each stroke. His canoe moved fast through the light swells when the first dolphin exploded out of the water. It cleared his head by mere inches as it crossed over to the starboard side and drenched him with seawater spray that flew off its body.

"Damn it, Koa!" Mike yelled at the dolphin as it circled the canoe. He was on guard now. He knew Kiki wasn't far behind and expected her to leap out of the ocean any second. Hopefully not over his head, as Koa had just done. That behavior was not typical of dolphins in the wild. But these two were not wild, or normal. They were highly trained, and they belonged to his brother Jack. According to the government, they belonged to the US Navy and were only in Jack's care. But, in reality, they were Jack's.

Mike made a mental note he needed to call his brother after he paddled and ask him if he could look into the problem neighbor. Jack had the resources to run a background check even though he had technically retired six months earlier from NCIS in Honolulu. Jack had moved to Kona to start a sport fishing business, but still worked part-time for the government doing contract work.

Mike felt there was something rotten about his neighbor Mr. Lau; it was a nagging feeling that just wouldn't go away.

But he knew Jack would find out if there was anything to be worried about.

Mr. Lau owned the Ming Resort next door to Mike's property and had made several offers to buy Aloha Village. Most people took no for an answer. Not Lau. The word *no* didn't seem to be in his vocabulary. Not even after Mike had told him, for the third time, that he was not interested in selling at any price. And certainly not so Lau could expand the Ming into a casino.

As Mike's canoe rounded Kaiwi Point, he decided it was time to paddle back to the pier. He needed to call Jack to see if he was back from Hong Kong yet.

After putting the canoe on top of his Tundra, he drove to the Old Kona Airport to chill at the beach while he called Jack. He parked by the first palm tree near the water and walked to the picnic table on the sand. He sat down on the bench and took a couple of minutes to watch the waves before he made the call.

After a few minutes of watching the waves, a thought popped into his head that maybe he should hedge his bet and call his daughter Jessica, too. He glanced at his watch and emailed her instead, he didn't want to wake her up because of the time difference between Hawaii and California. The email was short, he only asked her to call him when she had time. The more cops the better he thought as he clicked the send button on his phone.

Mike dialed Jack and got the answering machine. "Hey, Jack, call me when you get in. I need to talk to you."

A few seconds later his phone rang. He glanced at the number on the screen, he hoped it was Jack, but it wasn't.

"Aloha, Mike speaking."

"Howzit, Mike, this is Kimo, returning your call. You left a message yesterday. Are you still interested in the dive boat I have for sale on Craigslist?"

"Yeah, is it still available?"

"It is, but I got one guy that says he's coming to look at it later this afternoon. But you know how that goes. If you want to check it out, I'll be here all day today."

"Where's the boat located?"

"Hilo," answered Kimo.

"Okay, text me your address, and I'll leave right now."

"Shoots, brah, I send'm."

Mike needed to replace the resort's dive boat right away because it had a blown engine. Every day the boat didn't operate cost him income he couldn't afford to lose.

Kimo's boat was over ninety miles from Kona. Mike decided it was better to fly his plane to Hilo instead of driving. He could get there faster and check it out before the other potential buyer. He got up from the picnic table and dialed Kona Air Services as he walked across the beach back to his truck.

Kai Santos picked up the phone right away.

"Air Services, Kai speaking, how may I help you?"

"Howzit, Kai. Mike Murphy here. I need to banzai to Hilo real quick to check out a boat. Can you fuel my plane?"

"Shoots, brah, no problem. It'll be ready to go by the time you get here."

"Mahalos, Kai." Mike hung up the phone and headed to the Kona airport.

On the way to the airport, Mike's truck got a flat on the highway.

"Oh damn!" Mike said, as he realized he'd forgotten to put the lug wrench back in the truck after loaning it to a friend.

He waited for an hour for someone with the right size wrench to stop and help. That put him an hour behind schedule and in a huge rush to get to Hilo. He arrived at the airport and thanked Kai for having his plane fueled and ready to go.

After a thorough preflight, he sat on the taxiway, and

waited for clearance, from the tower, as the Gulfstream jet in front of him roared down the runway.

A minute later he heard through his headset, "November Hotel Juliet 224, cleared for takeoff."

"November Hotel Juliet 224 cleared for takeoff," Mike copied back to the controller and then applied full throttle and sped down the runway. The Beechcraft Bonanza lifted off and climbed above the lava field. At a little over three hundred feet, the engine died, and the plane stalled. There wasn't enough altitude to recover from the stall, and the small plane plunged straight into the lava rocks below. Mike Murphy died instantly in the crash.

2

JESSICA

Los Angeles

It was 2:12 a.m. when the phone on the nightstand rang. Jessica rolled over and grabbed it, while she squinted to see who was calling in the middle of the night. She was exhausted from the murder investigation she had just worked twenty hours straight to close. Jessica couldn't even focus one eye to read the screen on her phone. She opted to press the Off button and go back to sleep.

Twenty minutes later, she heard two loud knocks, like cops banging on the front door. "Crap. Go away," she grumbled.

She rolled out of bed, grabbed her .45 off the nightstand and stumbled to the front door. After a quick look through the peephole, she opened the door.

"Sorry to wake you, Lieutenant Kealoha, but the watch commander said it was important that we wake you up and tell you to call your sister in Hawaii. There's been an accident."

This wasn't good. She thanked the two burly street cops and closed the door.

Now wide awake, as the adrenaline flowed through her

veins, she picked up her cell phone and saw that her sister Pua was the one who called. She knew it must be serious. Pua never called her during the day, much less in the middle of the night. Jessica hit the redial on her phone as she paced the floor of her small apartment living room. Pua answered on the first ring.

"Jessica, there's been an accident," Pua said, as she sobbed.

"What happened, Pua?" Jessica asked softly.

"This morning Dad took off from the Kona airport and crashed his plane. He's dead. A witness said they heard the plane's engine sputter and quit, only a few hundred feet in the air. Then it crashed into the lava field, and Dad died on impact."

Jessica felt a sharp pain in the pit of her stomach, as if she had been kicked in the gut. Her knees buckled, and her eyes welled up with tears.

"I'll be on the first flight to Kona in the morning," Jessica said, in a complete daze.

After she hung the phone, she sat on the couch and thought about what Pua had just told her. She stared at a photo of her father that hung on the wall and wondered if the phone call from Pua wasn't real. Maybe she was in the middle of a bad dream, but it started to feel too real to be a dream.

For the first time in three years, she felt like taking a drink. But that was no longer an option for her. She took a minute to think through what would happen if she had a drink. Her next thought was "maybe tomorrow, not today."

She couldn't believe it. Her father, of all people, died in an airplane crash—it made little sense. He always took meticulous care of his plane. He was a perfectionist when it came to maintenance. Her father had been an engineer on the inter-island cruise ship for twenty years before going into the hospitality business. Nobody took better care of their airplane than Dad did. He knew better than anyone that equipment failure always seemed to happen at the worst possible time.

Something just didn't add up. How could this have happened? Was it sabotage? Who would want to do this? Her father didn't have any enemies as far as she knew. Maybe it was just an accident. He had been running the Aloha Village Resort at least ten years now. Jessica doubted anyone would want to kill him over something related to the resort.

Her mind raced and she needed answers.

3

GOING TO HAWAII

The flight from LAX to Kona took five hours and twenty-five minutes—a lot of time for Jessica to think. It was too soon to conclude that foul play had caused her father's death, but her gut told her there was something wrong. During most of the flight, she scribbled notes on her tablet about random thoughts and things she would do while back on the island.

Five hours after leaving LA, Jessica looked out the window of the 757 jet and could see the Big Island in the distance, her eyes started to well with tears. She always looked forward to coming home to the island, but not this time.

Twenty minutes later as the plane rounded the northern tip of the island the captain announced over the PA that they would land in Kailua-Kona in a few minutes. Jessica looked out the window at the turquoise ocean below, off the West side of the Big Island of Hawaii, it was as calm as a lake. That was typical of the leeward side of the island. The beauty from the air overwhelmed her, from the snow-covered tops of Mauna Kea and Mauna Loa to the extinct volcanoes of Kohala and Hualalai.

She saw a half a dozen fishing charters off the coast, most likely trolling for marlin. They reminded her of all the times she and her father would go fishing together. Just the thought of it caused her eyes to well up with tears again. A minute later, she pushed those emotions back down, just as she always did when she saw a disturbing crime scene involving a child. The other thing she could see was the lava flow where her father had crashed his plane and lost his life.

As the big jet was on final approach over the lava flow, she said a prayer for her father. She didn't believe there was a God that cared one way or the other, but she figured it never hurt to hedge your bet, just in case. If there was one, he had a lot of explaining to do as far as she was concerned.

Jessica texted Pua after the plane landed and taxied to the gate. _"I should be at the curb in a few minutes."_

As she exited the aircraft and walked down the ramp to the tarmac, she felt the warm, balmy breeze brush her cheeks. The scent of plumeria flowers nearby filled her nostrils. For a moment, she felt both sadness and relief at being back in Kona.

Kailua-Kona was a small town on the leeward side of the Big Island. Some of the locals referred to it as a drinking town with a fishing problem. It had the best blue marlin fishing in the world, and it was hot and dry compared to the other side of the island where Hilo, the county seat, was located.

Almost every day in Kona, it rained in the late afternoon above the eight-hundred-foot elevation. That also made it one of the best places in the world to grow coffee because of its unique weather pattern—early morning sunshine and afternoon showers.

***

Pua had arrived at the airport a few minutes early—uncharacteristically, since she ran late most of the time. She waited for Jessica, out front at the curb, in her new red Mercedes SUV as she listened to Bruno Mars and texted her broker about a real estate deal on the verge of blowing up. The other agent involved in the transaction had misrepresented the facts to her buyer. Pua's seller had told them to go screw themselves, once he'd figured out the truth, because of something the buyer had said during a chance encounter with the seller.

Pua always went first class; Louie Vuitton handbags, Vera Wang dresses, and the most expensive perfumes. She didn't care if she only had two nickels to her name; she wanted you to think she was wealthy by all outward appearances. But Pua was your typical real estate agent, broke one year and rich the next. From the looks of the new Mercedes, she had made bank for the moment, at least until the next downturn in the economy. She was a grasshopper through and through and could be a real diva. The ability to look the part made her feel like a high-end realtor. "Fake it till you make" it was her motto coming up in the early years of her business. And it looked like she'd finally made it since she only handled properties over a million dollars.

Jessica was a jeans and T-shirt kind of girl and could never understand how Pua had come from the same gene pool. It was just one of life's little mysteries that she had yet to figure out. When Pua saw Jessica heading toward the SUV, she got out of the driver's seat and waved at her as she walked around the back of the vehicle to the curb. Pua had on Maui Jim sunglasses to hide her puffy eyes, a tank top, jogging shorts and rubber slippers.

Who are you and what have you done with my sister? Jessica thought when she saw Pua. Grief—everyone had different ways of handling it, as Jessica knew from experience. Jessica was so good at hiding her emotions that no one could tell what was going on with her unless she shared it. But anybody that knew Pua could take one look at her and know something was terribly wrong in her world.

The two sisters had been ambivalent toward each other

their entire lives. After Jessica had stowed her carry-on bag, they hugged behind the Mercedes as if they truly meant it–for the very first time ever.

"Are you hungry, sis, or do you just want to go to the house?" Pua asked.

"I need a shower and some sleep," Jessica answered.

"Do you want to stay in my ohana, or do you want to go to Dad's?"

"I appreciate your offer. I may take you up on it later. But for now, I want to go to Dad's."

The sisters left the airport and headed north on the Queen Ka'ahumanu Highway to their father's bungalow at Aloha Village Resort. Hawaiian slack key guitar music played softly in the vehicle during the drive. The sisters didn't say a word to each other as they headed toward Aloha Village. After about ten minutes of silence between the two, Pua looked at Jessica,

"You don't think he did it on purpose, do you?"

Jessica shook her head.

"No. If he was still drinking, then I might consider that a possibility. Plus, I got an email from him before the accident."

"What did it say?"

"He asked me to call him and that it was urgent."

Pua looked at Jessica again. "Urgent?"

"He said he had a problem with a neighbor who wouldn't go away, and he wanted to talk about it."

"Mr. Lau," Pua muttered, as she shook her head.

Jessica's eyes narrowed. "Mr. Lau?"

The SUV came to a stop as Pua had parked in front of their father's bungalow and turned off the engine.

"One day when I was having lunch with Dad. His lawyer called, and Dad mentioned a Mr. Lau in the conversation. He was agitated when he got off the phone. He said the guy wanted to buy Aloha Village and kept making lowball offers.

He said hell would freeze over before he would sell it to that guy."

Jessica nodded and asked, "Did he ever say anything else about this Mr. Lau?"

Pua shook her head as she opened her door to get out of the vehicle.

After Jessica had gotten her suitcase out of the back of the SUV Pua said, "I'll pick you up later for dinner. I have something else we need to talk about then."

Jessica nodded and asked, "You want to come in for a little bit?"

Pua's eyes began to well with tears, "I can't go in there yet, and besides, I have a showing I need to be at soon."

Pua hurried to get back in her Mercedes before she started to cry.

4

HALE

As Jessica walked up the steps of the lanai that lead to the front door, she could feel her father's presence. Even though he wasn't there, she felt his spirit, and a warm feeling rushed over her as she walked through the front door. She felt the mana to her core. The house was neat, like he always kept it. The decor was typical Hawaiian style, with rattan wicker furniture and a canoe paddle hung on the wall in the living room. The front door had a Mako shark carved into it. Since the mana of the shark was important in Hawaiian culture, her dad figured it was a good omen for the place.

Mike Murphy was a no-frills kind of guy who loved Hawaii and its culture. But the one thing in his life he'd spared no expense on was his starburst-blue '69 Road Runner with a 426 Hemi sitting in the garage. He called it the BOAT, which stood for Bust Out Another Thousand. He was always installing some expensive new speed part to make it go faster. No doubt Mike Murphy was Kona's fastest grandpa. He was a racer at heart. It didn't matter what it was—cars, canoes, airplanes—he had to have a fast one.

The bungalow had two bedrooms and a huge bath with an

emerald-green granite countertop and matching floor-to-ceiling tiles. Early Hawaiian garage sale was okay for the rest of the house, but you would have sworn the bathroom was from the presidential suite down the road at the Hilton. But unlike the Hilton, the bungalow's jalousie windows allowed the cool ocean breeze to circulate throughout the house, with a smell of salt in the air that Jessica could taste.

She rolled her suitcase into the guest bedroom closet and fell backward on the bed. Too tired to put her things away, she wanted to take a nap before she saw her younger sister Jasmine. After she had lain there a few minutes, she realized something had been missing in the living room. Even though she was exhausted, her curiosity forced her to get up and go back into the living room. She looked around the room for a few minutes realized there were no photos of her mother anywhere in sight. Jessica thought it was strange but went back to bed and decided to let it go until after she had some sleep.

5

JASMINE

Jasmine was the youngest of the three sisters, and her father's right-hand man. He'd always thought of her that way, since boys had not been in the cards for the Murphy ohana and Jasmine ran Aloha Village for him when he was away. She had been at the beach all day, and filled in for the lifeguard who'd called in sick.

The day before, a shark had swum in close to shore and hung out in the small bay for an hour before it swam away. No one had seen it since, but Jasmine had told all the resort's guests to stay out of the water for at least twenty-four hours.

Once satisfied the shark had left the area for good, Jasmine removed the shark signs from the beach. It was almost the last thing she had to do before going to see her older sister, Jessica. But first, she had to inform all the guests that they could go back into the water.

Grayson Roderick, a stockbroker and first-time guest visiting from California, thought someone should have killed the shark at the first sighting, so as not to interfere with his snorkeling plan for the day. He'd complained when Jasmine had informed him that wasn't happening. She'd kindly reminded him that the shark was in its natural habitat and that it was them who had encroached. Mr. Roderick had grumbled something about going to Florida next time and walked away.

Jasmine thought she should have encouraged him to go to Florida next time, but bit her tongue. She was always friendly and professional with the guests, even the ones who should have been allowed to swim with the sharks.

Jasmine knocked on the door of her father's bungalow and waited. When Jessica didn't answer, she used her master key to open the door and stepped into the living room. Her father's golden retriever, Comet, waited behind Jasmine until she opened the door, then he shot around her and headed for the master bedroom still looking for Mike.

Jasmine heard the shower running in the back of the house and yelled out to Jessica to make sure she didn't startle her.

"I'm in the shower. I'll be out in a minute," Jessica shouted back.

Jasmine was hungry and checked the fridge while she waited for Jessica to get out of the shower. As usual, there wasn't a thing to eat. Her father never kept much food, if any, in the house. He always liked to go down to the resort's restaurant, the Marlin House, to eat and talk story with the guests. Comet came out of the bedroom and looked at Jasmine, perplexed. He didn't understand why Mike wasn't there.

Jessica came out a few minutes later with a towel wrapped around her. She hugged Jasmine and kissed her on the cheek. When Comet saw Jessica, he whined and jumped in the air, and spun in circles to let her know how much he had missed her. It had been two years since the last time Jessica had been home. She reached down and scratched Comet behind the ears just the way he liked it.

"How you doing, honey? Here, come sit by me on the couch." Jessica motioned to Jasmine as she headed toward it.

Comet thought the invitation included him too, and he jumped up on the couch.

Jasmine sat down and turned toward Jessica, "I keep hoping this is a nightmare I'm trapped in and I'll wake up from it. It doesn't seem real, though. I never thought about Dad leaving us until he was much older, and certainly not by accident. Maybe shot by a jealous lover or something." She grinned as she wiped the tears that started to flow. Jessica hugged Jasmine as tears streamed down her face, too.

Jasmine said, "Pua called me after she dropped you off and said she's taking care of all the arrangements for Dad. She'll be back here at 6 p.m. She also said she'd talk to you about something important later at dinner. I'll give you a heads-up, I think she's sick. One of my girlfriends I paddle with is a nurse at the Kaiser Clinic in town and acts weird now whenever she sees me. I sense something is wrong with Pua, and my friend can't say anything because of privacy laws. I'm worried about her. Please ask her what's going on for me, would you?"

Jessica pulled her arm back from around Jasmine's shoulder and pivoted toward her and said, "Let's not read anything into it. After I talk to her, I'll let you know what's up."

Jessica sat back on the couch and Jasmine curled up next to her, like she had after their mother died when she was very young. As Jessica softly stroked Jasmine's hair, she asked, "Where did the photos of Mom go?" Jessica had her arm around Jasmine's shoulder and could feel her muscles tense when she asked the question.

"Dad's girlfriend, Simmy, that's what happened. The woman's a complete nut job if you ask me. She was jealous of Mom's photos and asked Dad to take them down, but he refused. So one day, when he was out surfing, she removed them and wouldn't tell him where she hid them. I don't know what Dad saw in her. She was always accusing him of running around with other women."

Jasmine paused for a minute. "The woman was a scary kind of jealous about Mom's photos. I think Dad was planning to breakup with her but kept prolonging the inevitable drama that would surely follow once he told her goodbye."

Jessica lightly squeezed Jasmine's shoulder. "We'll find every last one of Mom's photos and put them back up. Now, let's get ready to go down to the Marlin House and see what's up with Pua."

6

MARLIN HOUSE

That night, the three sisters met for dinner at the Marlin House, they were greeted by lit tiki torches at the entrance and a breathtaking view of the ocean before they entered the restaurant. The Marlin House had eight foot tall hand-carved tikis on each side of the front door.

The foyer was a sizable, round room for dinner patrons waiting for a table. It easily held twenty people and showcased three blue marlins mounted high above on the wall outside the dining room. The biggest one was a world record holder and weighed thirteen hundred pounds.

Jasmine and Jessica arrived first and grabbed a table in the back of the restaurant. Jessica didn't like surprises, so she always sat with her back against the wall, and Jasmine didn't care either way. That night Bruddah Robert was played soft Hawaiian melodies on a twelve-string guitar, and his wife Lehua danced hula. It reminded Jessica of the Hawaiian music she had grown up with and how much she missed it after moving to the mainland years ago.

Twenty minutes later, Pua showed up late as usual with Kainoa, her twelve-year-old son. Born with autism, Kainoa was quite a handful sometimes. Pua didn't drink, but she had every reason to. Most of the time, Kainoa was pretty well behaved out in public, but once in a while he had emotional outbursts characteristic of autism and people would stare. And Pua would give them stink eye right back plus interest. She may have been a diva, but she was a good mother. Kainoa had played hard that day at school and decided to lie down in the booth next to Auntie Jessica. In less than five minutes he had fallen asleep.

Sam Stewart got up from his table across the room and walked over to offer his condolences to Mike Murphy's daughters. He wore khaki shorts, a Tommy Bahama shirt and a pleasant smile. His hair had a wisp of grey in it, and he sported a scar on the side of his neck that a pirate would have been proud of.

"I heard the news down at the harbor earlier today. And I'm so sorry for your family's loss. Mike Murphy had more aloha than anyone I know, many people will miss him."

"Mahalo, Mr. Stewart. These are my sisters, Jessica and Pua," Jasmine said, as she motioned to each as she said their name.

"Please call me Sam. Nice to meet you ladies. I'm just sorry it's under these circumstances."

Pua and Jessica nodded in agreement as they both shook Sam's extended hand.

"If there's anything I can do, please let me know."

Jessica smiled, as she took a mental picture of the tanned, handsome man looked directly at her.

He smiled ever so slightly, then returned to his table, and glanced up to meet Jessica's eyes once more as he sat down to finish his dinner.

Pua looked at Jessica and Jasmine, her eyes wide.

"Do you know who that guy is?" She could barely contain the amazement.

"All I know is he stays here from early November to late April or early May. But unlike a snowbird, he's from Southern California," said Jasmine.

Pua whispered, "He's one of the richest men in the world. He's the CEO of Stewart Industries and worth about seven billion dollars. I recall seeing him on the cover of *Stinking Rich* Magazine not that long ago." The three sisters laughed as they tried their hardest not to look in his direction.

Jasmine felt her phone vibrate in her pocket. She checked to see who called, there was a text a long message from the hotel front desk.

"Crap, I have to go," Jasmine said. "The front desk clerk says there's a problem she needs me to handle. Someone's demanding to speak to the manager. I'll be right back. Don't eat all the lilikoi pie without me." She smirked as she hurried off.

"No worries. I'm training for Ironman, so I can't have any right now," said Pua.

After Jasmine walked away and Jessica was sure she was out of earshot, Jessica turned to Pua. "Okay, cards on the table. Since when are you training for a triathlon, and what's going on with you?"

"What do you mean, Jess?"

"Jasmine told me earlier that she thought you might be sick and were keeping it from her. Are you okay?"

"I'm not training. I'm just not eating sugar anymore," Pua said, looking away for a moment.

Pua could never beat Jessica at poker. Her older sister knew all her tells—plus she was an expert interrogator. Jessica looked Pua straight in the eye. "You know lying to me is not a winning strategy, right?"

Pua stirred her coffee, looking down at the table for a minute before looking back up, her eyes full of tears.

"Jasmine is right–I have breast cancer. I found a lump

about six weeks ago and just got the test results back three days ago."

Jessica reached across the table and held Pua's hand, and caressed it. The tears welled up in Jessica's eyes too now. The waiter was approached the table but made a U-turn when he saw the two of them crying and hugging each other.

"I know you and I haven't been close, but I have a favor to ask, Jess. And it's not an easy one either. I need you to take Kainoa if I die."

Jessica nodded, then said, "You know I'm not exactly mother material, right?"

"Yeah, I know, but he'll be fine with you. I'm not the mother of the year, and he's survived so far," said Pua.

They both laughed and wiped away their tears with a fresh pile of napkins Michael had quietly brought to the table earlier.

"We have one more thing to talk about, Jess. You know how Dad was a great engineer?" Pua asked.

Jessica took a deep breath and exhaled, she sensed the bad news wasn't over yet.

"Yeah."

"The other side of the coin is he was never great at being a businessman. He always felt sorry for people, and he made bad business decisions over the last five years. So because he had such a big heart, the bottom line is–Aloha Village is almost broke."

"Yeah, well, let's sell it," Jessica said .

"We can't. I called Dad's attorney to get the ball rolling, and he said there's a problem. But he wouldn't elaborate on the phone. He said if we come to his office tomorrow, he'll explain the situation. I have to meet with a client tomorrow, I can't get out of it. Some rich guy who's only on the island for one day and wants to see a house I've been trying to sell for almost two years. I can't blow him off, the potential deal is too important. Besides, if I close this deal, I'll make enough money for you to take care of Kainoa until he's an adult if I die."

"Don't worry," Jessica said. "I'll take care of it."

She knew Pua always had a flair for the dramatic, but this time the danger was real, so she agreed to see the lawyer herself the next day.

7

JENNINGS

Jessica sat in the small foyer of the Kona law office alone and waited for her dad's lawyer to return from lunch. The secretary said he should be back any minute. Jessica passed the time by looking at photos of her and her father on her phone, taken on her last trip to Kona. She thought about the conversation they'd had about her moving back to Kona someday, after she retired from the LAPD.

She snapped back to the here and now as Mr. Jennings walked through the office door. He was short, fat and about two hundred years old–just like Pua had said.

He hobbled into the room and motioned her to follow him into his office and have a seat in the dark leather chair. Between the two of them was a big mahogany desk with a stack of papers, which the old lawyer picked up and shuffled through to find Mike Murphy's will.

"Are Pua and Jasmine coming?" Mr. Jennings asked Jessica.

"No, Pua's too busy with some big real estate deal and Jasmine has to run the resort, so it's just going to be me and you today."

"Jessica, your father left you, Pua, and Jasmine the Aloha Village Resort. He didn't leave much cash to go along with it. He had all his money tied up in the infrastructure of the property, and it's on the verge of bankruptcy. The good news is, your father controlled the master lease on the land underneath the resort. Selling it won't be a problem when the time comes, if you want.

"But there's a catch. If you and your sisters want to sell the resort, you'll have to renew the master lease first. That's the only way you'll get any money out of it. Mr. Lau, the owner of the Ming Resort next door, has made three lowball offers to buy the Village. He knew your father was nearly bankrupt. And he also knew the landowner trust wouldn't renew the master lease of the property if your father didn't bring the resort's buildings up to code.

"Your father wouldn't sell to Mr. Lau at any price because he knew he would ruin the Village. Your father viewed the island as sacred and fought to preserve it."

"Mr. Jennings, I have one question. Why didn't my father renew the lease now?"

"He didn't have enough money to make the infrastructure improvements the landowner required before they would renew. Your father could have borrowed the money, but he didn't want to be owing anything to anybody. Instead he was doing the improvements piecemeal as he had the money. He could be so stubborn sometimes," Mr. Jennings said.

Jessica smiled. "You're singing to the choir, Mr. Jennings. My father's middle name should have been stubborn."

"In the last few years, he had become a fierce adversary of mainland developers who came to the island and tried to turn it into Waikiki. Your father's guests at the Village loved him. Real estate developers hated him with a passion because he turned up at every county council meeting and fought them every step of the way. He wasn't going to let them pour concrete over paradise without a fight. I'm sure there's a long list of real estate developers that are glad your father is no longer around to fight them," Mr. Jennings said.

"Why does this Mr. Lau want to buy the property so bad?" Jessica asked.

"For one reason, its beach. The Ming's beach is full of lava rocks. If the Ming can take over your father's property, they can use the Aloha Village beach and bulldoze the rest of the place. And there is one more thing."

The old lawyer leaned back in his chair. "Something you should know about Mr. Lau. He's a Chinese billionaire from Macau, and he's been buying property all over Hawaii the last couple of years. I suspect he would like to turn the Ming and Aloha Village into a casino if gambling ever gets legalized here. He owns half the casinos in Macau and is looking to expand his gambling empire to Hawaii, from the news articles I've read."

Mr. Jennings sat straight up in his chair and looked Jessica in the eye. "He's connected to the Triads is what I've heard on the coconut wireless, so be very careful with this guy."

Jessica left the law office on a mission. Investigating Mr. Lau would be her new job while she waited for the NTSB report to come back with the cause of the crash. Mr. Lau had a motive, a means, and a good reason to want her father dead. If Jessica knew one thing for sure, there were people in this world that would kill for any reason to get what they want. And Mr. Lau had millions of them. If it turned out Mike Murphy's plane crash had been the result of sabotage, instead of an accident, he would be the prime suspect.

It was time to call Uncle Jack to see what he knew about this Mr. Lau.

8

MARLIN FISHING

After Jessica left Mr. Jennings's office, she drove out to the harbor to see if Uncle Jack was on his boat, the small fishing yacht he'd lived on since he'd retired. He didn't answer his cell phone, as usual. Jessica knew he had gone to Hong Kong earlier in the month, but she thought he should be back by now.

Uncle Jack had the connections to find out information she couldn't about Mr. Lau. Even though Jessica hadn't talked to Uncle Jack yet, she knew without asking that he'd be deep into the investigation of his brother's death by now. Uncle Jack, suspicious by nature, came from the Ronald Reagan school of "trust but verify."

Uncle Jack had retired from the Naval Investigation Service unit at Pearl Harbor. His life now pretty much consisted of going fishing and keeping an eye on Kiki and Koa, two dolphins trained by the Navy for special ops. The dolphins had come from a pod off the Kona coast of the Big Island of Hawaii before the Navy had trained them for special ops. After closing down its dolphin program in Hawaii, the Navy had returned them to the area and released them back into the wild.

Since Jack Murphy had a top-secret security clearance, the Navy had asked him to keep an eye on them, which consisted of monitoring their location via the GPS tracking devices the Navy had implanted in them. Little did the Navy know, Jack used Kiki and Koa to help him catch fish. When word got out, it kept Jack's charter business as busy as he wanted.

Jessica pulled up to the slip of the *Hui Hou,* Uncle Jack's thirty-five-foot Cabo. It surprised her to find Uncle Jack and Sam Stewart sitting in the cockpit drinking beer. What was going on here? But Kona was a small town; it wouldn't be unusual if they were friends or something. Maybe they'd gone fishing. Uncle Jack wasn't the only one in the family that was suspicious by nature. That was a trait that made them both such good investigators.

The *Hui Hou* had just come in from a half-day trip down to Red Hill to troll for marlin. Jessica checked herself in the mirror and touched up her lip gloss before getting out of the 4Runner. She walked toward the slip of the *Hui Hou* and waved at Uncle Jack and Sam as she approached the boat.

Jessica smiled and gave Uncle Jack a big hug and then gave Sam one, too. On the mainland, she would never have hugged Sam, but in Kona, it was the *local style* to hug even acquaintances in most social settings.

"Long time no see, Uncle," said Jessica.

"Well, that wouldn't be the case if you would move back to Kona," Uncle Jack said sarcastically. Sarcasm was Jack's specialty. Most of the time, he meant it in a good way–unless he didn't like you. Then he had a whole special brand of it.

"Did you guys go fishing today, or just drink beer and talk story?"

"Sam caught Old Smokey, but he got off the line. Just like he always does. Grab something to drink out of the cooler. There's plenty of stuff in there besides beer," said Uncle Jack.

Jessica opened the cooler and grabbed a can of cold Japanese green tea. She popped the top open and took a sip.

Sam looked perplexed. "You mean that fish had a name?"

"Yeah, as soon as he jumped out of the water, I could tell it was Old Smokey by the big chunk missing out of his fin, right next to the tag. I also knew you had a snowball's chance in hell of reeling him to the boat. Many a fisherman in Kona has tried to reel Smokey in, and none have succeeded. Except for one guy," said Uncle Jack.

"Who's was that?" Sam asked.

"My brother, Mike. He tagged Smokey and let him go."

There was a silence among the three for a moment, then Sam lifted his beer toward Jack and Jessica. "To Mike Murphy." And the three of them toasted.

"Jack, I had a great time fishing with you today. And, Jessica, it was a nice surprise to see you again. I'd stay longer but I have to head back to Aloha Village."

Sam shook hands with Jack and hugged Jessica. But this time there was something electric when they embraced. They both felt it. And they both tried to ignore it. Before getting in his rental car, Sam walked over to a plumeria tree and plucked a red blossom off a low-hanging limb. He took a moment to inhale the fragrance then turned and walked back to the *Hui Hou.* With a smile he handed it to Jessica, then turned and walked down the dock toward the parking lot.

She placed the flower above her right ear. "Thank you, Sam," Jessica said as he walked away. She stood still and watched him, and before Sam got into the car he looked back and smiled.

"Interesting," said Uncle Jack. Jessica smiled like she hadn't in a long time and ignored Uncle Jack. But there was something about Sam that drew Jessica to him whether she wanted to admit it or not.

"Are you ready for coffee? I picked up a fresh bag of roasted Makua. It's excellent," Uncle Jack said.

"Sure, why not?" Jessica said as her mind came back into focus.

"Follow me inside to the galley. I'll grind it up, and we can talk story."

When Jack opened the bag of fresh Kona coffee beans, the aroma filled the galley and saloon of the *Hui Hou*. Jessica and Uncle Jack both breathed in deep and sighed almost in unison as they enjoyed the heavenly fragrance.

In the galley, Uncle Jack glanced at Jessica and asked, "What's on your mind?"

"Earlier today, I went to see Dad's attorney concerning his estate," Jessica said, as she took a seat at the breakfast bar and sat up straight on the stool, as she watched Uncle Jack grind the coffee beans. "He told me some things that make me think we need to take a closer look at Dad's death. Are you familiar with Mr. Lau at the Ming next to the Village?"

Uncle Jack nodded, as he poured water into the coffeemaker. "Yes, he's been on my radar for a while."

"I don't suppose your trip to Hong Kong had anything to do with him, did it?" Jessica asked.

"I can't talk about it."

"I'll take that as a yes, then."

Uncle Jack pretended he didn't hear her and fussed about in the galley until the coffee was ready. Jessica moved to the couch. Uncle Jack followed with the coffee and sat next to her. He turned toward her, and looked her straight in the eye.

"I can tell you one thing for sure—my brother was obsessive about his airplane maintenance. The chances of him crashing due to a mechanical failure or pilot error are almost zero in my book. It's possible that's what happened. But I doubt it." Jack stared into his cup of coffee. "When do you go back to LA?"

"I'm here only until the paddle out, and then I have to go back and finish working a case."

"Do you still have contacts in the Kona PD?"

Jessica nodded. "Most of them I don't trust, but I have one that I do."

Uncle Jack finished the last sip of his coffee and stood up to take his cup to the galley. "Keep their number handy. We may need them. The last contact I had there retired."

9

SAM'S BUNGALOW

Bungalow number seven sat on the edge of the beach surrounded by tropical plants and flowers of every color, providing privacy. It had the best view of the ocean of all the bungalows at Aloha Village. Sam walked in and headed straight for the refrigerator, grabbing a cold beer. With beer and cell phone in hand, he went out front to the lanai, sat down on the chaise lounge and leaned back. He took a swig of his ice cold brew and looked out at the ocean, and relaxed while going over what just happened at the harbor–with Jessica.

It had been a great day of fishing on the *Hui Hou* with Jack Murphy. But meeting Jessica again had been the highlight of Sam's day. He loved her exotic look; half Japanese on her mother's side and half everything else on her father's, otherwise known as *hapa* Hawaiian. She was one of the most beautiful women Sam had ever seen. At first, he'd thought he should put his feelings aside and wait for a more opportune time to pursue a relationship. But then he realized life was short, and there was no time to waste.

Sam barely knew Jack Murphy; they'd only met once before because of Mike. Mike had talked about his brother working for the Navy as an investigator. But that was all Sam knew, other than Jack had retired, moved to Kona and started a charter business.

Sam had hoped he would learn more about Mike's death during the fishing trip. But Jack always played his cards close to the vest and didn't give up anything, so Sam wasn't too surprised. It had been worth a try, not to mention, he had almost caught a *grander*.

The story about Mike Murphy's airplane crashing on takeoff was all over the news, they all said it was an accident. But almost everyone who knew Mike suspected it wasn't. Even though Mike was in the hospitality business, he had made a lot of enemies over the years fighting developers from the mainland. Sam added his name to the list of nonbelievers and wanted to help the family, in any way he could, to find the truth.

Sam picked up his cell phone from the table and dialed his assistant in California. She answered on the first ring.

"Hi, Melissa, it's Sam, I'm coming back next week like I planned. But I'm not staying long."

"Oh? Is there anything you would like me to take care of before you arrive, sir?"

"Yes, put the house in Newport Beach on the market. It's time. I'll be coming to pick up the things I want from the house, and Mr. Jangles. If it were just the stuff, I'd ship it, but I'm not shipping the cat," Sam said.

"Anything else?" Melissa asked.

"Yes, donate all of Jamie's things."

"Are you sure?" she questioned.

"I'm sure," Sam said without hesitation. He'd never liked the Newport house much, but it had been Jamie's favorite, and he hadn't been ready to let it go until now.

Sam had just been going through the motions these last few years, he stayed busy with the day-to-day operations of his global empire. It had been five years since Jamie's death, and Sam had been alone all that time. He'd had no interest in other women until he'd met Jessica.

THE NEXT MORNING, Sam lay in bed and listened to the sound of the ocean and the chorus of exotic Hawaiian birdsong outside his bungalow. He propped his head up with two pillows and looked out at the ocean. The sea breeze flowed into the bedroom, past the open sliding glass door and flooded the space with the scent of gardenia.

After the nine minutes of meditation he always did first thing in the morning, he thought about his plans for the day. First, he'd take a morning swim in the ocean, and then he'd eat breakfast at the Marlin House.

When Sam walked in the front door of the restaurant, he headed toward his usual table in the corner. It surprised him to see Jessica already sitting there, sipping tea. Sam walked right up and sat down as if they had planned to meet. Jessica had her head buried in the newspaper, engulfed in a story about the Hawaii reefs dying from the effects of global warming, and didn't even notice Sam had sat down. When she looked up, their brown eyes met, and Jessica peered into Sam's for a moment as if two long-lost souls had reconnected.

Jessica said nothing. Sam smiled and said, "Good morning. I'll move to another table in a moment. I sit here every morning, but it's obvious you got here first. Unless you're willing to share?"

Jessica smiled back and then continued reading the paper.

"I'll take that as a yes," Sam said, as he picked up a menu. He didn't need to read it, he had it memorized and ordered the same thing for breakfast every morning. But he figured he'd hide his face in it until he could think of what his next move would be.

That morning, Loana was the server and walked up to their table.

"Good morning, Mr. Stewart. Mahi-mahi and eggs as usual?" she said.

"That would be great, Loana."

Loana disappeared back to the kitchen to put in Sam's request.

"Good thing you studied the menu," Jessica said as she folded the paper and set it down on the table. Her brown eyes looked straight at Sam, and she asked, "You knew my father well?"

"I did. We were good friends. We both liked boats and muscle cars. Your father and I would sit down at the Cast-away Bar and talk story for hours about who had the faster car or canoe. And this whole thing just makes little sense."

Jessica nodded in agreement.

"I'd like to help you find out the truth of what happened to your father in any way I can. While I'm not an investigator like you are, I do have something to contribute," Sam said.

Jessica's eyebrows rose a little. She wondered how he knew she was an investigator. She doubted Uncle Jack would have told him. Hmmm, maybe Jasmine.

Sam noticed Jessica's surprise and added, "Your father mentioned it a few times. That's how I knew."

"Sam, I appreciate your offer, but I work best alone."

Sam wasn't used to people telling him no. He thought for a moment and then asked, "Does that apply to your personal life too?"

"What makes you think I'm alone?"

Jessica took a sip of her tea as Loana came to the table with Sam's breakfast. Sam sliced into his fish, and just before taking a bite, he said, "No wedding ring. And I asked one of my spies here at the resort." Sam smiled as he chewed his fish.

The coconut wireless was one thing they didn't have when

she was in LA. There were no secrets in Kona. Everyone knew everyone, and they all seemed to know each other's business. She didn't miss that part of living in a seaside village one bit.

"What do you think about having dinner?" Sam asked.

"I have it most nights," Jessica answered, as she grinned.

"I mean us," Sam said with all the courage he could muster. This was difficult for him, and she wasn't going to make it any easier.

"It was nice to see you again, Mr. Stewart." Jessica stood up from the table to leave. "I'm sure you're a nice man, but I don't have time right now to get sidetracked. I have to find out what happened to my father." She grabbed her sunglasses off the table and walked out the front door of the Marlin House.

Sam couldn't believe he had just been shot down over what he thought was friendly territory. This just didn't compute. Women threw themselves at Sam all the time. He was the heartbreaker. Not the other way around. *Game on,* he thought.

10

SIMMY

As she made the short walk back up the hill to Mike's bungalow, Jessica thought about Sam. She felt there was something between them and wanted to explore that feeling more. But her priority was to handle her father's estate and find out the truth about his death. As she walked up to the bungalow, she saw a car parked in the driveway, and the front door was open. It appeared as if someone was loading the car with things from the bungalow. Jessica walked in the front door with a fair amount of caution and came face-to-face with Simmy, who attempted to carry a painting out the door. It was her father's favorite and had been in the family since Jessica was a child. Her father had gotten it on a trip to Japan, when he'd met Jessica's mother for the first time.

Jessica had met Simmy before and wasn't a fan. "Put it down, leave, and don't come back or I'll have you arrested for trespassing," said Jessica.

"Listen, bitch—"

Before Simmy could say another word, Jessica stepped behind her, grabbed her right wrist and swung it behind her back. She had Simmy by the neck and pushed her out the front door, just like she'd done a thousand times taking people to jail. Jessica slammed the door behind her as if she had just taken the trash out. Simmy got in her car and left in a cloud of burnt rubber, and spewed profanities out the window as she sped off.

Jessica called Jasmine. "Hi, honey, is Keoki still the handyman?"

"Yes," Jasmine answered.

"Send him up to Dad's place and have him change all the locks–today."

"I'll send him right up."

That moment Jessica decided she would fly back to LA as soon as possible and put in her retirement papers. There was no way she could leave Jasmine and Pua alone to deal with Simmy and run Aloha Village. And Pua would need her support while she battled breast cancer.

Cousin Keoki was full-blooded Hawaiian and a jack-of-all-trades at Aloha Village. Not only was he the resort handyman during the day, but he was also the fire knife dancer at the Friday night luau. It was a good thing that he was handy, since he'd almost burned the stage down during the show one time causing quite a commotion. He had flung the torch too high and it had landed on the stage's thatch roof. It had taken him two days, with a lot of teasing to repair the damage. After turning the stage roof into a tiki torch, his co-workers nicknamed him *the torch*.

Five minutes later, Jessica heard a knock at the front door, she opened it and smiled as she gave Keoki a big hug.

"Good to see you again, cuz," she said.

"You too, Auntie," Keoki said, and smiled back. "Jasmine said you need me to change the locks. Should I be on the lookout for anyone suspicious?"

"If you see Simmy, call the cops–then me," said Jessica.

Keoki scowled. "You got it. I never liked that woman much anyway."

11

PADDLE OUT

Mike Murphy's will stated that when the day came, there would be no memorial service on land. Instead, there'd be a Paddle Out, and his ashes would be scattered at sea. And just as he wished, about two hundred and fifty family and friends met at Kohanaiki Beach Park on a beautiful Saturday morning. At 9 a.m., they all paddled out past the shore break and formed a circle. Jessica, Pua, Jasmine, and Kainoa sat on their surfboards in the inner circle, floating in the sea like one big plumeria lei, surrounded by over two hundred people on boards or in canoes and kayaks, all draped with Hawaiian flowers of every color. With clasped hands and hearts, they shared memories and love, their joined hands were raised together. Mike's ashes were then spread in the circle along with hundreds of beautiful leis and flowers.

After a short prayer, an old Hawaiian friend of Mike's paddled out to the center and joined the daughters. "You are your father's legacy–do him proud. And going forward, know that his heart and memory kiss the shore with each wave. He will never be forgotten." He then hugged each one and they followed him back to shore as their eyes brimmed.

Afterward, there was a celebration in honor of Mike's life on the beach. No speeches, just people hanging out, grilling fresh fish and talking about the good times they'd had with Mike.

An hour later, a black stretch limo pulled into the parking lot near the beach. Two men got out of the car and walked down to the main tent on the beach to sign the guestbook and pay their respects to the family. The older man was Mr. Lau, the owner of the Ming Resort. He was in his late sixties, dressed in a five-thousand-dollar suit, and wore a poker-faced smile. It was obvious he hadn't gotten the memo this was a casual affair—or he didn't care.

Mike Murphy's family sat in the main tent and *talked story* with all the folks who had come to sign the guestbook and pay their respects. Pua knew Mr. Lau and introduced him to Jessica and Uncle Jack. They all shook hands and were cordial, as each tried to read the other's face. Except for Mr. Lau's bodyguard, Woo Ching, who stood silently off to the side with lips tight and glared at everyone. Mr. Lau's presence had little to do with paying respects–the gloves would come off soon enough on both sides.

After Mr. Lau and Woo Ching were on their way back to the limo and out of earshot, Jessica whispered to Uncle Jack. "Who was the creepy guy with Mr. Lau?"

"Funny you should ask that. I ran him through Interpol when he first showed up here a few months ago. His name is Woo Ching, he's Mr. Lau's nephew and personal henchman. He's also connected to the Triads in Hong Kong, and he has a rap sheet as long as your leg. He's a real nice boy," Uncle Jack said sarcastically.

"I don't suppose your recent trip to Hong Kong had anything to do with him."

But before Uncle Jack could answer, Sam walked up and greeted everyone.

Uncle Jack stood and said he had to get ready for a trip

back to Hong Kong. He put his hand on Jessica's shoulder and told her to have a nice trip if he didn't see her again before she returned to the mainland.

"No worries, Uncle. I'm coming back. I have to put in my retirement papers and clear out my apartment. Then I'll be back to help Pua and Jasmine."

Uncle Jack looked perplexed. "I thought you had to finish working a case."

"It's obvious my family needs me more than the LAPD," answered Jessica.

The sudden revelation stunned everyone. Even cousin Keoki, who was playing his ukulele, stopped strumming for a moment. No one had ever expected Jessica to move back to Kona.

Sam's eyes lit up, as he concentrated to contain his excitement. "Do you need a ride to LA?" he asked.

Jessica glanced at Sam, a puzzled look crossed her face.

"I'm going to LA myself, and I have a plane here," Sam explained.

"That's very generous, Sam, but I'm fine with the red-eye," Jessica replied.

"We can leave at night if that'll make you feel better," Sam said. Everyone laughed, even Jessica, who was always too serious. And to sweeten the deal, Sam said, "No TSA, and no long lines to wait in to board the plane, unless you're a fan of that."

Uncle Jack put his hand on Jessica's shoulder and whispered in her ear, "Sam is a good man. Accept his offer, and I'll tell you about Hong Kong when you get back."

"Okay, Uncle. I'm trusting you to keep your word," she teased.

Uncle Jack smiled, hugged Pua and Jasmine and then left to go pack for his trip to Hong Kong.

Jessica didn't want to give Sam the wrong idea; she still wasn't interested in a relationship. Not because she didn't like

Sam, but because she was on a mission to find out what happened to her father. After that, who knew? Maybe she would think about it–maybe.

"Okay, Sam, I'd love to hitch a ride. When do you plan on leaving?"

"How about tomorrow morning? The plane is always ready to go. Meet me at Air Services at about 10 a.m.?"

Private jets and traveling on a whim wasn't the world Jessica lived in, but it sure sounded inviting and definitely more comfortable. Putting in her retirement papers would be bittersweet after twenty-one years on the force. And moving back to Kona could be just the thing to fill the void in her life.

12

LA

The next morning, Jasmine drove Jessica to the airport. When they pulled into the parking lot, Sam was already there, and stood out in front of the office, next to the Air Services shuttle, talking with Kai Santos, the FBO manager.

Jessica hugged Jasmine a little longer and harder than usual. "I'll be back in a week." Jasmine beamed a big smile, nodded, and then drove away.

"Howzit, Jessica," Kai said. "Long time no see."

He knew her from high school, they'd both attended Konawaena at the same time. "Aloha, Kai, you look good," she said as she walked toward him and Sam.

Kai smiled and said, "Thanks, it's from paddling every day after work."

Sam opened the side door of the van, smiled, and with a grand gesture, motioned to Jessica. "Please, after you."

Kai drove them out to the Gulfstream jet on the ramp and wished Sam and Jessica a safe trip. As they walked up the short staircase of the plane, Sam placed his hand on the small of Jessica's back. His touch sent a warm feeling up and down her spine, something she hadn't felt for a long time.

Once on board, Captain Mike Johnson stood in the doorway next to the cockpit and greeted Sam and Jessica as they entered the plane. "Good morning, Mr. Stewart. Good morning, ma'am."

"Good morning, Captain. This is Ms. Kealoha." Jessica smiled and shook his extended hand.

"Winds are light today. Flight time is five hours and four minutes, sir,"

"Giddy up, Mike." Sam said with a grin.

Ten minutes later the Gulfstream jet climbed out of Kona, and made a right turn over the sparkling blue ocean, as it headed toward the US mainland.

Jessica sat buckled into the soft leather chair next to Sam and looked around the cabin. *So this is what it's like to be a member of the wealthiest one percent.*

"If you want to take a nap, there's a button on the side of the chair that will recline your seat flat, converting it into a bed," Sam said.

"I'd like that. I didn't get much sleep last night."

Twenty minutes later, as she slept, Sam got a blanket out of the closet and carefully covered her with it. She briefly woke up when she felt the blanket touch her skin and saw Sam's outline through her squinting eyes. For a moment, before she fell back asleep, she thought about how quickly she could get used to a lifestyle of being cared for by a man.

Sam had hoped he would get to know Jessica better on the flight to California. However, she'd slept almost the entire trip and didn't awake until just before they landed at John Wayne Airport in Orange County. It was the first time she had slept over three hours in a row since her father's death. She felt safe with Sam, and started to think she wanted to be with him–sooner than later.

Security was always a concern when Sam was anywhere else in the world besides Kona. And because of that, after they'd landed, Captain Johnson taxied to Sam's private hangar. This allowed Sam and Jessica to depart without the prying eyes of the tabloids' mercenary photographers. The last thing Sam wanted was to have Jessica scrutinized in the press. That was the benefit Sam loved about living in Kona part-time—the anonymity that came with it. Nobody cared what you did on the mainland or how famous you were there.

Inside the hangar were two black Ford Expeditions with dark-tinted windows, each with a driver who stood nearby. After Sam and Jessica walked down the staircase of the plane, he pointed to one of the SUV's and said, "The driver will take you anywhere you want to go."

He handed her a piece of paper. "This is my contact info, if you need anything, just call."

Sam spread his arms out to hug her goodbye and she warmly embraced him as she fought the urge to lift her chin up and kiss him on the lips. It just felt so–right. But not now she thought as she quickly released him and briskly walked to the nearest vehicle.

As instructed, the driver took Jessica to her apartment in Anaheim, it was just a few miles from Disneyland. She didn't care much for Anaheim, but she liked going to Disneyland at least once a month. It was, after all, the happiest place on earth, at least according to the marketing. But it was a nice contrast to the ugliness she witnessed daily, investigating murders. She enjoyed watching the families interact, the children's excitement and the laughter.

13

WEEK LATER

Before making up her mind to go to LAX, Jessica again fought the urge, this time to call Sam and hitch a ride back to the Big Island on his plane. She needed to focus on her father's suspicious death and not battle her hormones all the way back to Kona, as Sam sat next to her. He had become more desirable each time she saw him but she didn't have time for distractions. At least that was what the business side of her brain told her. It was in contrast to what her emotions whispered in her ear, *go for it*.

It had been a busy week for her. She had put in her papers, said her goodbyes, and packed up her apartment. There was nothing left to do except go back to Kona, and the logic overruled her heart's desire for Sam for the time being and she caught the afternoon United flight out of LAX.

The funny thing about Kona was that it was such a small town, it wasn't unusual to see people you knew on the plane. Although Jessica had been away for many years, she'd been born and raised in Kona and still knew a lot of people there. While she waited in the lounge, to board the plane, she recognized Sonny Palio. Their eyes met at the same time, and it was obvious by the look on his face, he recognized her too.

Annoyed with herself for not looking away sooner, she now felt obligated to talk with him when he beelined over to strike up a conversation. He was an old boyfriend, and as they chatted, it became evident why their relationship hadn't gone past three weeks in high school.

Their short conversation went something like, "Now that you know what *I* think about me, what do *you* think about me?" he said, with a grin. What had she been thinking back then? Hormones were the only rational explanation.

After they had boarded the plane, she sat about sixteen rows away and tried not to look in his direction for the entire flight. He stopped by her seat to chat once more while he was on the way to the bathroom and said they should get together in Kona. Ugh. Did that mean for coffee, or did he think he'd just asked her out on date? Men were funny; you never knew what was going through their brains. Most of the time it had something to do with their penis doing the thinking. She smiled. The other thought she had was that she now regretted she had not called Sam for a ride back to Kona.

That was one thing she'd miss about the big city: the anonymity that came with it. Going to the store and not recognizing a soul—there was comfort in that sometimes. But right now, her family needed her more than ever. She would have to put her personal preferences aside for the time being.

SAM HAD ALSO BEEN VERY busy. He'd signed the documents for the sale of the Newport house and was ready to move on with his life after five years of being alone.

He had his businesses programmed to run by themselves. He liked setting them up, but he didn't care to run them on a day to day basis. He would always find a key employee to take over. And when possible, he would pick one who came from the humblest of backgrounds because he just liked helping people succeed. The next venture he had in mind was an inter-island ferry system in Hawaii.

Sam had always lived near the ocean and felt a connection to it. The next step would be to call the governor of Hawaii to arrange a meeting to see if he would smooth the regulatory process. Hawaii was just like any other place; it wasn't always what you knew, it was who you knew. The backroom deal was alive and well in the Aloha State.

Sam called Melissa. "I need you to call the Hawaii governor's office and set up a meeting."

"What should I tell him it's about?" asked Melissa.

"I want to start an inter-island ferry. And I would prefer not to spend five years in court with the conservationists before getting started."

"I'll take care of it and let you know when I have a date for the meeting," Melissa said.

Sam had one more phone call to make. "Hey, Mike, it's Sam. Meet me at the airport tomorrow morning at ten. It's time to go back to Kona."

"10 a.m. tomorrow. Roger that," Captain Mike said.

It bummed Sam out that he hadn't heard from Jessica during the week they were on the mainland. But he was patient; he knew they would be together in due time. All he needed to do was convince her of that.

14

RETURN TO KONA

As soon as Jessica landed in Kona, she turned her phone on and it pinged with a dozen text messages. One of them was from Uncle Jack. "We have to talk." *Rather cryptic,* she thought.

Six hours earlier, before she boarded the plane, she had called Pua and asked if she could pick her up at the airport. Pua had agreed and said she'd be parked in front of the airport. When Jessica reached the curb, she found Jasmine waiting for her instead.

"Where's Pua?" Jessica asked as she put her suitcase in the trunk of Jasmine's Kona Cruiser, a yellow '85 Toyota Tercel.

"She's sick. She asked me to come get you," said Jasmine. Jessica's momentary annoyance evaporated, and was replaced by guilt.

Jessica asked Jasmine to drive straight to the harbor first so she could see Uncle Jack. When they arrived at the slip, the *Hui Hou* wasn't there. He must still be out on a charter, Jessica thought. As they were got ready to leave, she saw the *Hui Hou* come around the point. Uncle Jack and another man, that Jessica didn't recognize, were the only ones on board.

Jessica asked Jasmine to wait in the car and said she'd be

back in a few minutes. Jasmine was content with that, since she'd be able to resume texting with a guy she'd met online the day before and planned to meet for a drink later.

"Hey Uncle, I got your text," Jessica said, as she walked up to the boat.

"Where's Sam?" he asked, with a curious look on his face as he secured the lines from the dock.

"California? I don't know. It's not my day to watch him. Anyway, what's up?"

Uncle Jack looked down at the deck as he rinsed it with the freshwater garden hose from the dock. Then he looked up and said, "Did you see that guy that left the boat?"

Jessica nodded.

"He's the lead NTSB investigator assigned to your dad's crash. I've got a friend in the FAA who knows him. My friend got me an off-the-record phone call with him, which led to an off-the-record day of deep sea fishing on the *Hui Hou*. He found sugar in the gas tank of your dad's airplane. The sugar plugged up the fuel filter, which prevented the engine from getting fuel and caused the loss of power that resulted in the crash."

Jessica gritted her teeth, "I knew it, my gut told me it wasn't an accident."

Jack nodded. "Let's keep this to ourselves for now. The NTSB report won't come out for months. We might as well use that to our advantage and figure out who did this before they're even aware we're looking for them."

"Agreed," Jessica said, with clenched fists.

Uncle Jack and Jessica had both started out in law enforcement in Kona. They knew there was a fine line separating a few of the cops and the criminals on the island. Some Kona families had their fair share of both—including the Murphy ohana.

Uncle Jack had finished rinsing the salt water off of the exterior of the boat and started to wipe it down as he talked.

"I'm doing a contract job for Homeland Security right now because of my extensive contacts in Hong Kong. The Triads operating in California never worried the feds too much, but them gaining a foothold in Hawaii is a different story. They are serious gangsters with ties to the Chinese government. What's interesting about this is that these guys have never operated in Hawaii—until now. There's more to it, but I can't talk about anymore details because it's classified. But what I can tell you, is it's related to the Chinese government." Uncle Jacked threw a towel to Jessica, so she could help wipe down the boat while they talked, and then continued.

"I can't go any anywhere near Mr. Lau. My boss says he's off-limits. I'm not sure why, but I have my suspicions. So you'll have to see if you can interview him. I'll work the back channels and do what I can to help, but you'll be the lead dog on this Jessica," Uncle Jack said.

The sound of a car horn interrupted the conversation, and they both turned toward the parking lot and as Jasmine leaned out the window of her old Tercel. "Eh! I got places to go," she yelled and flashed a smile.

Jessica held up her index finger and turned back to Jack. "Okay, Uncle, I get 'um," Jessica said with a pidgin tone that meant business.

Jessica and Jasmine threw Uncle Jack a shaka, as they left the harbor and headed back to Aloha Village. Jasmine had a hot date with a guy she planned to meet at the Ming's bar. And Jessica had a hot date with the bathtub at her dad's place. An hour's worth of soaking in the tub to think about what Uncle Jack had said, was next on her agenda.

15

BREAKFAST

The following day at the Marlin House, Sam arrived half an hour early to claim his table. Like most people, he was a creature of habit and liked to have a morning ritual. The rest of the day, he could wing it. But mornings were sacred to him, and he wanted things just so.

Jessica liked the table at the Marlin House where Sam always sat because it had one of the best views of the bay. But she wouldn't do what he had done the last time. No, she'd pick a different table to sit at and get to work, to think only about the next step in the investigation. A seaside romance was the last thing she wanted while she investigated her father's death, but every time she saw Sam her armor weakened a little more.

When she arrived for breakfast at the Marlin House, she saw Sam sat at the table she'd hoped to get. She wanted to ignore him and headed to the opposite side of the restaurant, but she stopped and went back to his table so she could thank him for the ride to California and the car service.

Sam reiterated that if there was anything he could do to help find out what had happened to Mike, he was more than willing, all Jessica had to do was ask. She thanked him for his offer but politely conveyed that she doubted there was anything he could do to help. She was the homicide cop. He was the rich guy. What could he bring to the table?

***

Sam had finished his breakfast and sipped coffee as he stared at the ocean from his table when his cell phone buzzed. He glanced at the screen and saw it was Melissa. He picked up the phone and said, "Good morning, Melissa."

"I got you an appointment to meet Governor Fitch on Thursday at 9 a.m. and you won't even have to go to Honolulu. He'll be in Kona to play golf at the Ming that day. He said he could meet you there at the clubhouse for a few minutes before his tee time."

Governor Fitch's willingness to meet so soon didn't surprise Sam. Hawaii was the "You scratch my back, I'll scratch yours" state. The governor knew Sam wanted something, and he also knew Sam could contribute considerably to his reelection campaign if the governor could give him what he wanted. That was one thing about being a billionaire; people always took your phone calls.

Before Sam left the Marlin House, he walked over to Jessica's table. "I'm meeting with the governor on Thursday, at the Ming, if you'd like to tag along. He might be of some help with your father's accident investigation."

Jessica had a mouth full of loco moco and couldn't talk, but she nodded just before Sam turned and walked away, just as fast as he had approached the table.

She didn't have any desire to meet the governor, but she wasn't going to pass up an opportunity to go next door and chat with Mr. Lau. That night she called Sam to confirm that she would like to go with him to the Ming on Thursday.

16

GOVERNOR

Sam picked up Jessica Thursday morning at 8:30 and they shared a golf cart ride over to the Ming next door. They hadn't crossed paths the last couple of days because Sam had been out with Pua, and had looked at properties to buy. He liked staying at Aloha Village, but it wasn't a long-term solution. If he moved to Kona, he would buy a place.

"Pua showed me a ninety-acre coffee farm yesterday that I liked a lot. It even comes with two dogs." Sam said, with a grin.

"It comes with dogs?" she questioned, surprised at what he said.

"Yeah, the owners haven't been home in six years, and they want to leave the dogs with the only place they've known as home. The dogs think the caretakers are their masters, anyway, since the owners haven't been back. No need to rock the boat, I guess, if I buy the place. Besides, I like dogs. Speaking of boats, I'm thinking about starting an inter-island ferry,"

"You know you'd have a better chance of going to Mars first, right?"

Sam turned his head from the golf cart path and looked at her for a moment, with a gleam in his eye. "Yeah, I know. I like a challenge, what can I say?"

She was starting to see why Sam was so wealthy. He had big ideas, and he went after what he wanted. She didn't want to discourage him, but she thought she should at least warn him that getting a ferry going in Hawaii would be a lengthy battle.

"I think the ferry is a wonderful idea. But you'll have a fight on your hands with the people on Maui and Kauai. Hire a lot of lawyers. You'll need them."

It rolled right off Sam's back, he threw his head back and laughed. "Somehow I don't doubt it for a minute."

* * *

Governor Fitch was a short, heavyset man with a beard, a bad toupee and an agenda. He was at the Ming to play golf with Mr. Lau and discuss when the gambling law in Hawaii would change. Fitch wanted to legalize gambling, and he also wanted to get re-elected. Lau had put close to a million dollars into his reelection campaign through various phony shell companies so they could both achieve their goals. And the way Lau saw it, he owned the governor, and he wanted the gambling law changed sooner than later.

Sam and Jessica arrived at the Ming's Hibiscus Room at 9 a.m. to meet with Fitch. Lau hadn't planned to stick around—that was, until he saw Jessica was with Sam, then he made it a point to stay.

Governor Fitch and Sam stepped off to the side of the room to keep their meeting private. Lau took the opportunity and asked Jessica if he could show her around while the two men talked. She agreed, and they stepped into the room next door, where there was a mockup of a proposed extension to the Ming. It showed the Ming as one big resort, with the grounds of the model extended to include Aloha Village.

After she'd looked at the model for a minute, and noticed

a proposed golf course where her father's bungalow sat, Jessica had to fight to keep her composure. She shoved her feelings aside and listened to Lau talk about his plan for the Ming. With no emotion on her face, she looked him squarely in the eyes and remarked, "I notice your model encompasses our resort."

Lau smiled. "This would be the plan, if we could come to an agreeable price for Aloha Village at a later date. I don't expect you to make any major decisions about Aloha Village, right now, so soon after your father's passing," he said solemnly.

Sure, you don't, she thought with a half smile on her face. She returned to the Hibiscus Room to see if Sam's meeting with the governor was over.

Fitch and Sam had just finished up. They shook hands, and Sam said, "Thank you so much for your help today."

The governor smiled. "It was a pleasure doing business with you, Mr. Stewart."

Sam and Jessica headed back to Aloha Village in their golf cart. She was silent as Sam drove through the lush grounds of the Ming that lined the path back to Aloha Village. She held a plumeria flower to her nose that she had picked up before she'd gotten in the cart. It contrasted the anger felt that radiated through her body.

Since the governor was on board with Sam's plan to start a ferry, Sam was all smiles. Except for the fact that it would require a significant campaign contribution to the governor's reelection fund. Sam hated to pay politicians to get them to do their jobs, but he looked at it as a necessary evil of doing business.

"So what did you and Mr. Lau do in the room next door?" Sam asked.

"He told me about his plans to destroy everything my father ever worked for. Other than that–it was a great time."

Sam noted her clenched jaw and didn't say anything else.

As a homicide detective, nothing bothered her at work except dead kids. But this was different. This was her family, and she had a hard time suppressing her feelings. Her father had fought the mainland developers for years to keep Kona from becoming like Honolulu. She understood her father's love of Aloha Village and the people who came to work and play there. And for some Chinese gangster to come in and build a golf course on top of what her father held sacred, the thought of that was unbearable for her.

After a period of silence, Jessica asked Sam,

"Why do you want to start a ferry system? Wouldn't a cruise line or something else be more profitable with a lot less headache?"

It didn't take him more than a second to respond, "After the first billion, making money gets boring, and you look for ways to help your fellow man instead. Well, at least some of us do when we get to that income level. And besides, I already own a cruise line." He grinned and looked at Jessica.

Until now, Jessica didn't care for rich men. All the perks that came with them were nice, but there was a lot of baggage that went along with that. In high school, she had worked part-time jobs at various resorts on the Kona Coast and had been hit on by a lot of wealthy men. Most of them were married and looking for something on the side. She could see that wasn't the case with Sam. And with that, another *chink in her armor* fell on the path, as she rode back to Aloha Village.

Unlike the others she had known over the years, Sam appeared to be the real deal. A good guy with a good heart. She'd grown rather fond of him, even though the circumstances of their being together right now were not what she would consider ideal.

* * *

After Jessica and Sam left, the governor and Lau sat at the private bar inside the Ming.

"Well, did you make her an offer?" the governor asked Lau.

"No, but I let her know an offer was on the table at a later date if she would like to sell."

Governor Fitch narrowed his eyes and puffed out his chest. "If she doesn't accept the offer, let me know. I'll figure out a way to impose eminent domain so you can take possession of Aloha Village and build the casino, once gambling is legal." He raised his whiskey glass in a toast and continued, "No worries, my friend. We will get control of that property, and one day we'll have the largest casino in the state."

Each man smiled and as they drank, their thoughts of power were more intoxicating than the liquor.

17

PUA CANCER

Jessica sat on the lanai of her dad's bungalow, and stared at the ocean. Comet's head lay on her lap, as she rubbed his ears and listened to the surf crash on the beach. Her mind had aimlessly wandered when the phone inside the house rang and jolted her out of the trance. She couldn't believe her dad still had a landline.

She gently nudged Comet off her lap, she went into the kitchen and grabbed the phone off the counter. She glanced at the caller ID and saw it was Pua. She felt a twinge of guilt in her gut. She had paid no attention to her sister since she had gotten back to Kona. "Hey, sis. How are you feeling these days?" Jessica asked quietly.

"Like I've been beat with a stick. I suspect in a hundred years from now, people will look back at how we treated cancer patients and think how barbaric it was."

"I'm so sorry, honey. I know I haven't been there for you–that changes today," Jessica said, and slapped herself on the forehead.

"No worries, I know you've been busy trying to figure out what happened to Dad."

Jessica appreciated that her sister understood but felt guilty just the same.

"I thought I'd give you a heads-up. Uncle Jin's coming over to visit. He heard you were back and called to say he wants to talk to you. But didn't elaborate," Pua said.

Jessica went from guilty to annoyed and tapped her fingers on the counter. "I see he still has eyes in Kona," she mused. "I don't want him on the property. Hell, I don't even want to be out in public with him. Tell him we'll meet at your place, if that's okay with you."

"Sure, you guys can meet here, he likes coming here anyway. He's been a good uncle to Kainoa the last few years. I hope you two can set aside your differences."

Jessica frowned but held her tongue and decided to change the subject. "Do you have plans today? Can we hang out?"

"Who are you, and what have you done with my sister?" she teased. They both laughed.

"I have plans to show your new boyfriend, Sam, some property today,"

"He's not my boyfriend," Jessica answered, in a flat tone.

"Okay, if you say so. But I've seen how you look at him." Pua seemed to take pleasure in teasing Jessica. Pua continued, "You're welcome to tag along. I'm sure he won't mind. Besides, maybe you'll want to go into real estate now that you've retired from the force and you can see what *A Day in the Life* is like."

Jessica knew Pua trying to be nice, but the thought of selling real estate was the last thing on her mind. "Okay, it's a deal," she said and hung up the phone.

Pua called Sam and asked if he minded Jessica tagged along for the day when they went to view property. He was almost giddy with excitement at the chance to spend the day with her. He had two properties he wanted to look at. One was up mauka, it was a coffee farm at a higher elevation, and the other was ocean front at Keauhou Bay. He liked them both but decided he would let Jessica pick which one he bought, though he wouldn't let her know she had the deciding vote. If their relationship progressed to the next level, she would eventually live there someday.

18

HOUSE HUNTING

Mike Murphy's bungalow sat on a hill which overlooked the entire Aloha Village Resort and the ocean. As Jessica sat on the lanai she could see Sam as he walked up the long driveway toward the bungalow. "Aloha, Sam," she said, as he neared the lanai.

"Aloha, good morning. It's a beautiful day in Hawaii," he answered with a big smile.

Jessica stood up and walked down the three steps of the lanai to give Sam a hug. After the warm embrace, she handed him a small gift box she had waited to give him.

"What's this?" he asked, as he shook the box.

"Just a little something for your generosity. Open it."

He untied the bow and opened the box. Inside was an exquisite hand-carved fish hook necklace made of koa wood and tipped with cow bone. "It was my father's. He would have wanted you to have it, and I want you to have it, too."

"I'm honored, thank you." Sam slipped the necklace over his head. Jessica reached over and turned the hook to point toward his heart. "There, that's better. That's how it's supposed to be."

Sam reached into the pocket of his aloha shirt and pulled

out a yellow plumeria flower. He gently placed it above her right ear and bent to kiss her on the cheek, but before he could she turned her mouth toward his. Their lips met for the first time and, at that moment, she knew it was fate–she couldn't fight it any longer.

Momentarily surprised, Sam placed his hands on each side of Jessica's face. Cradling her cheeks as he looked deeply into her eyes. She met his gaze, just as intensely. Both smiled, knowingly, as Sam's hands moved to her lower back and pulled her into his body, Jessica wrapped her arms around him. They kissed, as it was their last, with an urgency too long denied. After several minutes, Jessica giggled and pulled away. "Pua will be here very soon. "All right—I almost forgot," Sam said, and laughed. Jessica grabbed his hand and led him up to the lanai. "This day's turned out to be better than I anticipated—way better," Sam said, as he grinned.

They sat next to each other on the lanai swing and took turns as they rubbed Comet's ears. They rocked back and forth, in rhythm to the bliss and contentment each felt, as they waited for Pua.

When Pua arrived, and saw Sam and Jessica sitting on the swing together, she noticed something was going on between the two of them. Jessica had a glow to her face that Pua had not seen in years. And Sam, well–grinned like a Cheshire cat.

AT THE SECOND PROPERTY, Sam and Jessica stood on the lanai and leaned on the rail, and took in the magnificent view of Keauhou Bay. They watched the warm tropical ocean lap at the shoreline, as yellow tangs swam by the front of the estate.

"Which place do you like better?" Sam asked. "The coffee farm was nice and the view of the entire coastline was spectacular. But the view here is also spectacular, and you can be in the water in seconds, just like at Aloha Village."

Jessica's face lit up as she pointed toward a low-flying pueo over the bay. "There's your answer. The owl is sacred in Hawaiian culture. It's an omen."

It was clear to Sam she liked the place on the water better. He decided, at that moment, that he would make an offer. Now if he could just get over his fear of sharks, he might consider swimming in the bay.

Pua interrupted their private moment. "What do you think Sam?"

"Make a full-price offer."

"Okay, but there's something you need to know that just came to light. When I was in the house on the phone a minute ago, I was talking to the seller's agent and she told me that there'd been an offer made about 10 minutes ago." Sam didn't bat an eye. "Call her back and tell her whatever the offer from the other side is, we'll top it by hundred thousand dollars."

Pua frowned. "I'm told the seller accepted the offer."

Sam didn't like being told he couldn't have something. "Tell the seller's agent that I'll pay the buyer a hundred thousand to walk away, and I'll give the seller a hundred thousand more than the offer they accepted."

"I'll make the offer," Pua said. As she turned and smiled knowing it was a done deal.

19

UNCLE JIN

Uncle Jin Tanaka was the boss of the yakuza in Hawaii. He was a major reason Jessica had moved to the mainland twenty-one years ago to continue her career in law enforcement. It would have been impossible for her to remain on the job in Kona because of her sense of duty.

The police suspected Uncle Jin was responsible for a majority of the organized crime in the Hawaiian Islands. She knew a lot of cops who looked the other way when it came to the yakuza and family, but she would not be one of them. She didn't like the thought of being under constant scrutiny, with half of her family being Japanese gang members—or the prospect of having to arrest one of them someday.

It was quite the family tree. On her father's side, federal agents and cops, and on her mother's side, Japanese gangsters. It always made for interesting conversation at the Thanksgiving dinner table.

Both federal and state law enforcement agencies suspected Tanaka of having ordered half a dozen murders in Hawaii over a thirty-year period. But many people thought of him as a humanitarian as he supported various local charities and causes. He was a pillar of the community on both Oahu and the Big Island because of his contributions over the years according to local civic leaders—at least, the ones he hadn't tried to extort money from. Half the people who knew him thought he was a saint, and the other half suspected he was the devil himself.

The FBI had tried for years to get enough evidence against Tanaka to go to trial, but they could never infiltrate the yakuza. And since the murders were of some of Oahu's most unsavory characters, the cops had done the minimum amount of investigation and called it a day so they could move on to more pressing issues–like seat belt enforcement.

Pua picked up Uncle Jin at the airport just as she had every other Saturday for the last two years and brought him to her house, where Jessica waited. Kainoa loved his uncle and looked forward to his frequent visits, especially since his father had long since abandoned him. Uncle would take Kainoa to the beach, where they would play in the surf for hours and then get shave ice.

Kainoa was excited as always to see Uncle Jin and ran up and gave him an enormous hug, when he walked in the door with Pua. "Go beach, Uncle?" he asked with a huge smile on his face.

"Soon. I have to talk to your Auntie Jessica first."

Kainoa's smile melted as Pua grabbed his hand and led him back to his bedroom. She didn't know what Uncle wanted to talk with Jessica about, and she didn't want to know.

Jessica sat at the kitchen table, sipped coffee, and watched him–she didn't say a word. Uncle Jin filled a cup of his own and sat down across from her.

They stared at each other for a moment before she asked, "So what do you want to talk about?"

He smiled. "That's what I love about you, kid. You get right to the point. So I'll do the same. You have a problem."

"Yeah, I know—you for a relative," Jessica snapped back.

Uncle Jin ignored her comment. "The governor and the Triads are planning to take control of Aloha Village."

"How?" Jessica asked.

"My source tells me Governor Fitch is looking to take the resort by eminent domain if you refuse Lau's next offer."

Jessica took a sip of her coffee and studied Jin's eyes as she swallowed the hot liquid before asking, "Why are you telling me this, and why do you care?"

"Because the Triads are trying to take over Hawaii, and we can't let that happen."

"We?"

"Like it or not, we must work together to fight the Triads and the governor. I've heard rumblings that the Chinese government is behind them and may have plans for Hawaii."

Jessica pulled a piece of gum out of her purse and bit down on it. "Me, work with you, the yakuza? Remember the last time that happened? You went to prison. And do I need to remind you that my father's side of the family puts your side of the family in jail for a career?"

Uncle Jin smiled. "I know that. I also know you held back in court. Or else I'd still be in prison."

"Let's just say grandfather kept you from getting a life sentence. And if there ever is a next time, you're getting the max if it depends on my testimony."

Uncle Jin Studied his niece's face for a moment and then nodded and continued, "If the Triads and the governor get their way Kona, as we know it, will cease to exist. There only needs to be one Waikiki in Hawaii and the Big Island will eventually look like Honolulu if they get their plans approved."

Uncle Jin took the last sip of his coffee, got up from the table and walked over to the sink to rinse the cup.

"As much as I'd like to save Hawaii from the Triads and

its governor, I don't have time. I'm more interested in finding out who killed my father."

Uncle Jin ignored Jessica's sarcasm and looked out the window over the kitchen sink at the ocean as he spoke. "I'm almost sure Lau gave the order to sabotage your father's airplane."

"How do you know? Do you have any evidence?" Jessica's posture straightened.

"One of my people works at the airport and saw Woo Ching come out of your father's hangar the night before he crashed his plane."

Jessica said nothing. She sat there and stared at her uncle and wondered how much of what he said was true. What was really in it for him? There was no love lost between him and her father. She doubted he cared one way or the other about her father's death–or her, for that matter.

Her father and Uncle Jin weren't enemies—Mike was the only Murphy who hadn't been in law enforcement. But just the same, they weren't friends either. It was Uncle Jack that Jin hated. He was the one responsible for sending Jin to prison. Unlike Jessica, Uncle Jack had done his best to lock up Uncle Jin for as long as possible. Now that Uncle Jack was living in Kona, Uncle Jin kept a low profile when he came to the Big Island and saved all his nefarious activities for Oahu. He only came to Kona to act as a big brother for Kainoa and check on a couple of businesses he owned in town that were fronts to launder money.

The thing about Uncle Jin was that he had respect for the old Hawaii that Mike Murphy had fought hard to protect from mainland developers and people like Lau. He also was no fan of Governor Fitch, who he had been paid off for years to leave the yakuza alone on Oahu. If he could get Lau put away for Mike Murphy's murder, that would be one less competitor in the crime world of Hawaii. And if he could get Jessica to do all the work, that would be even better.

"Okay, Pua, were done," Jessica called out.

Pua and Kainoa returned to the kitchen just as Uncle Jin and Jessica were walking toward the front door.

"Which beach are you guys going to?" Pua asked Uncle Jin.

"The Ming," he answered.

"Their beach sucks. Why are you going there?"

Jessica interjected, "He's going over there to mark his territory."

Pua shook her head. "I should've known."

Uncle Jin said nothing, but grinned as he grabbed Kainoa's hand to leave.

"Hey, Uncle, have him home by six, okay?" Pua said. Uncle Jin waved his hand as he got into his car.

"Did you two have a good talk?" Pua asked.

"Not so much good–as very interesting,"

Jessica replied, as she watched the car until it turned at the corner down the street.

After Uncle Jin and Kainoa had left, Pua came back inside the house and joined Jessica at the dining room table.

"We should go diving tomorrow morning. The surf is flat and visibility should be good."

Jessica nodded and said, "That sounds like a good idea if you feel like you're up for it."

"Right now I'm between chemo sessions and I feel pretty good, so let's do it. And besides, my doctor said whenever I can spend time in the ocean swimming is good exercise. And hopefully we'll see dolphins."

20

PUAKO

It was 6:30 a.m. when Jessica arrived at Pua's house; she was still half asleep and Pua was buzzing with excitement. "We'll stop at the dive shop and pick up two tanks, then head up to Puako, if that sounds good to you." Jessica nodded as Pua handed her a cup of coffee before they climbed into Pua's truck.

Red and pink sun rays filled the sky over Mount Hualalai as the sun rose behind the mountain. It was a gorgeous morning, Hawaiian slack key guitar music filled the cab of the Toyota Tacoma as they cruised into town to pick up their scuba tanks.

After a brief stop in town, the sisters cruised north on the Queen K Highway, as the locals liked to call it, to one of their favorite dive spots in Puako.

After about twenty miles, Jessica asked Pua, "What happened to all the coral graffiti on the lava flows?"

"Some group of self-appointed do-gooders, with a lot of time on their hands, deemed it an eyesore and removed it. Now people just use spray paint to write on the lava. I don't know why people can't just live and let live."

"Look, it's so clear you can see Maui," Jessica said, as she pointed at Mount Haleakala in the distance.

"Yeah, the volcano has mellowed out the last couple of years, and we have a lot more clear days now," Pua replied.

After a pleasant drive along the Kona coast, they arrived at Waialea Bay in Puako. They got out of the truck, stood on the sandy beach and wiggled their toes in the sand as they watched the two foot tall waves roll for a while before they put on their wetsuits and scuba gear.

They did a quick safety check of their gear and discussed their dive plan before they snorkeled out to the drop-down spot.

That day, the surface of the ocean was flat, it looked more like a lake. The underwater visibility was excellent at eighty plus feet. After they had dropped down thirty feet below the ocean's surface and swam along the reef, Jessica felt her body relax for the first time in a long while. Ah, zero gravity is a beautiful thing, she thought. It felt so good to get back in the ocean again.

As she swam along she noticed the reef looked healthy, with lots of tropical fish and a sea turtle here and there.

A few feet away, Pua played with an octopus she had found that tried to blend in next to a coral head. She handed it to Jessica so she could feel its soft, velvety skin.

About that time, a dolphin swam up from out of the deep and went right up to Jessica. The poor creature had multiple fishing lines wrapped around it that cut into its fluke and needed help to remove the tangled mess.

Jessica and Pua both worked at a quick pace to untangle and cut free the fishing line that tortured the poor creature. It was unbelievable how patient the dolphin was, it rolled over right in front of them so they could cut away the line wrapped around it.

After they freed the dolphin, it gave them both what

appeared to be a smile and swam off into the abyss, gone just as fast as it had appeared.

Pua and Jessica stared at each other for a minute in total disbelief. It was a moment they knew they would never forget, and they savored every minute as they swam along the reef, and thought about what had just happened.

Jessica looked at her air pressure gauge and signaled Pua she was low on air. She pointed up toward the surface, and Pua signaled back okay.

As soon as the sisters broke the surface, it became obvious they were in big trouble. While they had been down below, a freak storm had blown in. The ocean surface had gone from calm to large swells in less than an hour. Six-to-eight-foot waves pounding the shoreline, getting back to the beach would be dangerous.

Jessica pulled the regulator out of her mouth and yelled at Pua over the sound of the wind, "I don't know about you, Pua, but getting pounded into the reef wasn't in my game plan today."

Pua had surfed on the women's pro tour in her late teens and early twenties and could make it through the big surf. But Jessica always stayed on the beach when the surf was over eight feet. This surf was far bigger than any she had ever bodysurfed, and to swim through it with dive gear on, was the last thing she wanted to do.

Pua dropped her weight belt and took off her BCD. Then she unstrapped the scuba tank and let it drop to the bottom before she put the BCD back on to use as a life jacket. "You have to drop your tank," she yelled at Jessica.

Jeez, Jessica thought, *we're really going to do this.* She followed Pua's instructions and dropped her gear in forty feet of water, and watched it sink to the bottom.

"No turning back now, Jess. Let's go."

The good news was that at least they had fins on. The bad

news was an even bigger set of waves rolled in, twelve to fifteen feet in height.

"Let's try to bodysurf in," Pua yelled. Jessica nodded in agreement as the next gigantic wave came rolled in. They both put their heads down and swam as fast as they could to catch the wave.

Pua was a much stronger swimmer than Jessica and caught the wave and rode it all the way to the beach. As she crawled up to the beach, she looked back to see where Jessica was. When she didn't see her, she threw off her BCD and ran back into the surf to find her sister.

Jessica swam just slow enough that she hadn't caught the fifteen-foot rogue wave but had gone over the falls, as the surfers called it. Because she'd been late to catch the wave, she'd been at the top of it when it had crashed onto the shallow reef and knocked her out.

Between waves, Pua found Jessica as she floated facedown close to shore. She grabbed one of the straps on Jessica's BCD, flipped her over, and swam as fast as she could with one arm. She kicked her fins harder than she ever had in her life. If she didn't, they would get pounded on the reef by the next wave, and that would be the end of them.

Pua dragged Jessica's head and chest out of the water and onto the beach just enough so she could start CPR. Jessica's lips were blue–every minute counted.

"You're not dying today!" Pua yelled at Jessica, as she pumped her chest.

Thirty pumps and two breaths were all Pua could remember to do for CPR. It would have to work, because Pua's energy had faded fast and she was ready to collapse.

About two hundred and fifty yards down the beach a nurse, who was visiting the island and taking photos, saw what was going on. She ran up to help and took over the CPR.

"It's okay, honey. I called 911 as soon I saw what was going on," the nurse said.

Sam had planned on meeting Pua and Jessica after their dive so they could all go to Cafe Pesto for lunch. When they weren't at the boat ramp at the agreed-upon time, he scouted around the area to look for them. Fifteen minutes later, he found Pua's Tacoma parked on a side road near the beach, so he stopped to see if they were nearby.

Sam rounded the corner from the road to the beach, and saw Pua with the nurse huddled over Jessica's body in the sand, about a hundred feet away. He knew it wasn't good and broke into a run toward them.

"What happened? Where're the paramedics? How can I help?" Sam fired the questions at Pua.

"Call 911 and find out where the hell the paramedics are," the nurse barked, as she pumped Jessica's chest.

Sam pulled out his phone and made the call. The operator said the paramedics were on the way, but some kind of equipment issue had slowed them down.

"What about the fire department helicopter?" Sam asked.

"It's out of service for repairs," the operator answered. Annoyed did not begin to describe the look on Sam's face.

Sam called Uncle Jack. Fifteen minutes later, a Black Hawk helicopter from the Pohakuloa Training Area, just east of them, landed in a clearing near the beach and flew Jessica to the Kona hospital.

21

HOSPITAL

Six hours later, Sam, Pua, Uncle Jack and Jasmine sat in the hospital waiting area. Nobody said a word until Dr. Kiyoshi came into the room. They all jumped to their feet, sounding like a group of reporters as they fired off one question after the other. "How is she? Is she going to be okay?"

Dr. Kiyoshi smiled. "She'll be fine. She's awake now. We want to run more tests and keep her overnight. You guys should go home and come back in the morning to pick her up."

Everyone shook Dr. Kiyoshi's hand and broke down into tears and hugs. Even Uncle Jack showed signs of a tear or two.

Pua had to get home because of Kainoa. Jasmine had to get back to running the resort. Uncle Jack had to go explain why he'd used a marijuana eradication helicopter to save a civilian. And Sam had resolved to stay in the waiting room until Jessica was ready to go home.

The next morning, a nurse came in and woke Sam, who had slept the night in a chair. "You're waiting for Jessica Kealoha?"

Sam nodded as he sat up and rubbed his eyes.

"We'll bring her out in a few minutes and you can take her home."

Sam stood, stretched, yawned and waited until Jessica came through the double doors in a wheelchair. Jessica had hoped it was Sam waiting for her, and she couldn't have been happier to see his smiling face. Although he looked like he had been through the ringer after sleeping in the waiting room all night. He had a five-o'clock shadow, bloodshot eyes, and disheveled hair. Not his typical put together look–Jessica loved all of it.

Sam wanted to hug Jessica, but she put her hand up to stop him. "There's nothing I would love more than a hug from you. But I have two broken ribs from all the fun I had yesterday."

Sam recoiled as if from a hot flame. "I'm so sorry, honey." He then reached down, caressed her hand and kissed it. "I almost lost you. Never do that again. Okay?" His eyes welled with tears.

* * *

As Sam and Jessica drove along Mamalahoa Highway, Jessica didn't take the view for granted. The plumeria flowers along the highway were more beautiful that morning than they had ever been before, the ocean bluer and the salt air more soothing. Nothing like being dead yesterday to make one grateful to be alive today. And for Sam, having almost lost Jessica made him even more determined to enjoy every minute with her–from that day forward.

"Pua has been working on getting the house at Keauhou Bay. I wish it were ours now. I mean, ready to move in. I'd just take you there." Jessica looked at Sam for a second with admiration and then looked back toward the road as they drove through Kainaliu toward Kailua Town.

Jessica reached over and rested her hand on Sam's thigh. "If you don't mind, I'd like to stop at the old airport."

"Sure."

Jessica sighed. It was nice to be taken care of for once.

"I'd just like to sit on a picnic table underneath one of the naupaka trees and watch the surf for a little while before going home."

And that was what they did. They sat like two geckos on a pineapple for an hour, and stared at the ocean. They watched the surfers catch waves, then get barrel rolled and glide all the way to the beach, as if on a magic carpet.

She thought about what had happened the day before, how the sea had taken its best shot at her and had come up short. But she knew she had been fortunate. Jessica didn't view it as any god looking out for her. Getting slammed onto the reef was just bad luck; wrong place at the wrong time. It was as simple as that. Or at least that was her first thought; she had decided a long time ago that there was no God. And if there was, He didn't seem to care about people, as evidenced by all the rotten things that happened in the world.

Sam said it was *obvious* someone or something had looked out for her. The nurse who'd been on the beach, in the right place at the right time. Uncle Jack had access to a helicopter by making a phone call. The most senior ER doctor was on duty at the Kona hospital when she arrived. Sam didn't believe in coincidences. He believed everything happened for a reason. They were opposites when it came to their view on whether or not there was someone or something behind the scenes overseeing things. Jessica had never wavered in her beliefs before, but she had started to reconsider.

They sat mesmerized at the picnic table, watched the surfers rip up and down the waves and the fishing boats cruise by. "Yesterday when I was on that beach not breathing, I had an out-of-body experience. And the funny thing about it? It was okay if that was how it would end. But the paradox was, I wasn't ready to leave yet. It must have been my sense of making things right that pulled me back. My father's murder cannot go unavenged. And if I don't bring the person responsible for his death to justice, I might as well have died."

Before Sam responded, an HC 130 Coast Guard plane flew overhead, as it scanned the ocean. The only time you saw them in Kona was when someone was having a dreadful day. And for the first time in years, Jessica said a short, silent prayer for whoever the Coast Guard was looking for–just in case it turned out that it mattered.

22

HOMECOMING

Sam took Jessica back to her dad's bungalow where everyone gathered, on front on the lanai, waiting for her arrival. There must have been fifty people who waited to greet her and share aloha. It looked like a gathering at the courthouse; most of them were cops, and two were Jessica's yakuza uncles. Jessica looked at Sam, as they drove up the driveway, surprised by the crowd.

"Know anything about this?"

Sam shook his head no and grinned.

Only in Hawaii was what came to mind when Jessica recognized all the people she knew. They were from both sides of the legal fence; those who enforced the law and those who broke it.

Sam parked the truck and announced to the crowd, "No hugs, she has two broken ribs." He opened her door and slowly helped her out of the truck and up the steps of the lanai to an empty chair.

For the next hour, Jessica's family and friends showered her with love, and leis, to let her know how glad they were that she was still with them and hadn't been taken by the sea.

After everyone left, including Sam, Jessica went inside.

There was a message on the answering machine from Mr. Jennings's law office. It said that Mr. Lau had made another offer to buy Aloha Village, this time for full retail value, in spite of all the work the property still needed to have done. Jessica called Mr. Jennings back and told him Lau couldn't buy Aloha Village–at any price.

She didn't care how much money he offered. Just like her father, she would never sell it to him. Especially now that she knew Woo Ching had been spotted at the airport, exiting the hangar Mike kept his plane in, and was suspected of causing her father's death.

23

STAGE FOUR

Jessica called Pua the next morning to set a lunch date for later that day at Kona Inn. It was Kona's oldest watering hole and a favorite of Jessica's since she was a little girl. The old fans that hung from the ceiling and the koa wood canoe over the bar were remnants of days gone by in Kona.

She realized after her near-death experience that it was time to put the living first. While it was important to bring her father's killer to justice, spending time with Pua became her top priority. She didn't know if Pua would survive the cancer, and it was time for her to set aside their differences.

When she and Pua arrived at Kona Inn later that day, the song "Over the Rainbow," by Brother Iz, played throughout the restaurant at a low volume, and Jessica felt a sense of well-being she only experienced when she was in Hawaii.

The two sisters sat at a table on the outdoor patio next to the three-foot-high rock wall closest to the ocean. It had an unobstructed view of Kailua Bay and the tour boats as they came and went from the pier. A few minutes later, a middle-aged waitress approached their table. She had a friendly smile and a beautiful plumeria flower above her left ear.

"Aloha. Would you ladies like something to drink?"

"I'll have iced tea," Jessica said.

"I'll have the same," Pua answered.

After the waitress walked away, Pua asked Jessica. "Are you still on the wagon?"

"Yeah, something like that."

"How long has it been this time?"

"In dog years?" Jessica smiled, then her expression turned serious. "Three years, two months and six days. But who's counting?"

"Way to go, sis."

"Thanks."

"Do you still go to AA?"

"When I can, sometimes the job gets in the way. So far, so good, knock on wood."

"In your case, knock on wood and go to meetings," Pua said with a serious tone.

Jessica nodded and smiled just as the waitress returned with their iced teas.

As they sat on the lanai and sipped their drinks they took in the view of the swaying palm trees and turquoise bay, with small, white-crested waves breaking along the shoreline, fronting Kona Inn.

They watched two young local girls play in the surf at the small beach across the bay, next to the pier, just like they had when they were kids. The trade winds blew, and that kept the humidity to a pleasant level. It was almost a perfect day weather wise.

Jessica didn't want to ask, but she had to know. "Did you get the PET scan results this morning?"

The grim look on Pua's face gave Jessica her answer. "On the way here my doctor called me. It's not good. The cancer has spread to my liver." She picked up a napkin and dabbed her eyes as they filled with tears.

Unlike when she had been told Marlin House, of Pua's

cancer, Jessica attempted to not cry–she needed to be strong for her sister.

"Take it one day at a time. It'll be okay."

Pua dabbed her eyes again with her napkin and nodded. "The doctor says he wants to take out part of the liver."

Jessica scooted her chair over next to Pua and put her arm around her shoulder. For a few minutes they didn't say a word, they just watched the canoes that paddled in Kailua Bay, that readied for the weekend races. Jessica's phone buzzed in her purse, as it broke the moment of silence. She glanced down and saw it was Mr. Jennings's number and decided she better take it. "Hello, this is Jessica."

"Hi, Jessica. I got your message declining Lau's offer. I wish you would reconsider. Finding another buyer willing to pay full price for Aloha Village in its current condition will be hard, if not impossible."

"The answer is still no, Mr. Jennings."

She hung up the phone and continued to rub Pua's shoulder, which she had lightly squeezed as she talked on the phone.

"What was that all about?" Pua asked.

"Lau made a full-price offer on Aloha Village. But I told Jennings to tell him that it's is not for sale–at any price."

"You didn't feel it necessary to run that by Jasmine and me first?" Pua snapped.

"Do you want to sell it to the man who's most likely responsible for Dad's death and would turn the Village into a casino?" Jessica countered.

"If you weren't here, I'd sell that place right now and be rid of that nightmare. It's a never-ending money pit, and the sooner we're out from under it, the better."

Jessica didn't react; she didn't want to get into an argument in public about the property. She knew it would get back to Mr. Lau and the less he knew about the Murphy ohana, the better.

"I'm just trying to do the right thing here," Jessica said quietly.

"Have you considered asking Sam if he'd be interested in buying or investing in the resort? Or what about Uncle Jack? Dad alluded more than once to Uncle having made a lot of money investing in stocks."

Jessica hadn't thought about Uncle Jack. The only thing she knew for sure was that she would not ask Sam for the money, to save anything. Nothing made couples fight more than money and relatives. Then the thought crossed her mind, *We're a couple?*

Jessica wasn't optimistic by nature. She believed that what could go wrong, would go wrong most of the time. She knew this wasn't a healthy way to think, and she fought it daily. But this time, she knew in her heart everything would be okay–all of it. Pua, Aloha Village and her relationship with Sam. Nothing like a near-death experience to get your attitude about life straightened out, she thought.

"We need to form a partnership to buy the resort," Jessica said, with excitement in her voice. "What do you think?"

Pua chewed on a cold French fry for a minute, and thought about what Jessica had said, before she answered. "Maybe we could get Uncle Jack to invest."

Pua and Jessica were so excited they drove out to the harbor to see if Uncle Jack was in port, since he didn't answer his phone as usual. They couldn't wait to pitch him their idea to save the Village.

24

UNCLE JACK

Uncle Jack sat in the fighting chair on the deck of the *A Hui Hou,* as he read the local fishing news and puffed on a cigar, when Pua and Jessica drove up. *So much for peace and quiet,* he thought when he saw Pua's truck park in front of the *A Hui Hou's* slip.

"Hey, Uncle," Pua and Jessica called out as they walked down the dock toward the boat. Uncle Jack didn't know what to think. He couldn't remember the last time he'd seen those two together–and happy about it.

"For someone who was almost dead a couple days ago, you look pretty good, Jess," Uncle Jack said.

"Let's say I'm re-energized," Jessica said, and flashed a grin.

Pua never minced words or wasted time when money was involved. She told Uncle Jack what they had in mind about forming a partnership of investors to save Aloha Village. Since real estate was her thing, Jessica kept her mouth shut and let Pua talk, while she nodded at the appropriate times.

"I think it's a noble idea. But I'm broke. You know the old cliché—*'if you want to be a millionaire in Hawaii, bring two million with you.'* A month ago, I paid off the boat and its slip because I didn't want any payments when I retire for good."

Pua and Jessica both looked like they'd had their balloons popped.

"But, I think I know where you can get the money. If I were you, I'd call an employee meeting at the Village and pitch them the idea of making all the employees part owners," Uncle Jack said.

"Dad paid them well, but I don't think he paid them that kind of money," Pua said. The optimism on Jessica's face had disappeared.

"You're right. But one of the aunties, that teaches lei making to the guests, is from a family that owned half of Honolulu until a few years ago. When they cashed out during the last real estate boom, each family member walked away with about three million dollars each. She doesn't work at the Village because she has to, she does it to share the aloha of old Hawaii with the visitors. You could skip calling a meeting, and just ask her, but you never know, there might be others working there that have some money stashed away who would want to invest."

25

EMPLOYEE MEETING

All twenty-three Aloha Village employees gathered Saturday morning at the beach for the meeting. Most of them had worked at the resort for over twenty years, and it was more like a working ohana than what most people would consider a job.

Jessica started the meeting by thanking everyone for their years of service and then got right to the heart of the matter.

"Aloha Village is broke. We can't borrow enough money to fend off foreclosure. The owner of the Ming next door wants to buy us and expand his property to include a casino almost on top of where we're standing."

Auntie Loana had worked at the Village since the early seventies. She stood up and said, "No can!" with a thick pidgin accent.

Jessica nodded in agreement. "We won't sell the Village to them at any price. But we have a problem. We need to sell to someone, and the Village isn't in sellable condition right now. We want to form a partnership to fund the resort going forward and would like to offer you guys the opportunity to be in charge of your destiny."

Auntie Loana stood back up. "How much you need, sista?"

Jessica looked Auntie in the eyes. "We need at least five hundred thousand to buy us some time. Or a little over a million to finance repairs, then get the trust landowner to renew the lease for another twenty years."

"Only a million? Shoots. Can handle." And with that and a huge smile, the old Hawaiian woman sat back down.

Jessica couldn't believe what she had just heard. Nobody knew Auntie Loana had that kind of money. She had been driving the same Kona cruiser to work for the last ten years. It was an old faded red '83 Toyota Tercel. Other than one gold bracelet that said "Ku'uipo." By all outward appearances, she didn't look like she had two nickels to rub together.

"Okay, we all work for Auntie now," Jessica said. Everyone laughed and one by one, each person hugged Auntie Loana.

After the meeting, Auntie Loana got out her checkbook and wrote a check for one point two million dollars. She'd included a couple hundred thousand extra, just in case the resort needed it. As she handed Jessica the check, she said, "This is a loan. I don't want to own the Village. You pay me back when you can." Jessica and Pua both had tears of gratitude in their eyes.

"Wait until Monday to deposit. I need to move the funds from my investment account on the mainland to the local bank." Jessica and Pua looked at each other in amazement. They'd never dreamed Auntie Loana was this sophisticated, secret millionaire.

"Okay, Auntie–Monday," Jessica answered.

26

DECISION

After the phone call from Mr Jennings, which relayed Jessica's message that the Village wasn't for sale at any price, Mr. Lau decided that Jessica must be eliminated if he was going to be able to buy Aloha Village. It was clear she was just as stubborn as her father had been and would never sell the property to him.

With Jessica out of the way, Lau was confident that he could persuade Pua to sell.

Lau had a spy who'd worked at Aloha Village, for the last year, who had instructions to report anything that would help the Triads take control. When he got wind of the beach meeting, he called Woo Ching into his office. "I need you to take care of a problem for me. Be sure that Ms. Kealoha does not reach the bank Monday morning." Woo Ching nodded and left Lau's office without a word.

Woo Ching was the Triads' most notorious hit man in Hong Kong and had been sent, to the Ming in Kona, for just such an occasion as this. His preferred method of choice would be a car bomb. He would never be able to plant it on Jessica's 4Runner while it was parked in the Village. So the next best thing was to bury the bomb alongside the road, leaving the resort. Woo Ching would wait until he saw the 4Runner on the road to trigger the bomb with a cell phone detonator.

27

THE HIT

At eight thirty on Monday morning, Jessica sat on the lanai of her father's bungalow, and had her morning tea. The trade winds had blown all the haziness out of Kona the day before, the sky was so clear she could see Mount Haleakala on Maui in the distance. The birds chirped, and the surf broke against the shoreline—a welcome change compared to her mornings in California. When she looked out the window of her apartment in Anaheim, all she saw was a fenced-in patio with two dead plants. She couldn't keep them alive no matter what she did. And everywhere she looked, when she was at work in the city of Los Angeles, all she saw was death. She didn't miss it for a second.

As she daydreamed, a yellow plumeria flower blew onto the lanai from a nearby tree and landed near her feet. She sat her cup of tea down on the table and reached over to pick up the flower. She admired its beauty and held it close to her nostrils, she breathed in the sweet aroma of the flower.

Her phone buzzed on the table, and interrupted her early morning serenity.

"My car has a dead battery. I need to take the 4Runner to town this morning," Jasmine said.

Jessica twirled the stem of the plumeria between her fingers. "The keys are in it. I have to go to the bank today as soon as you get back, so don't dally, okay? On second thought, never mind. I'll take Dad's Road Runner to the bank. You can keep the 4Runner all day if you need to."

"Okay, thanks, I'll come get it."

Ten minutes later, as Jasmine drove on the road that led from the Village to the highway, she came upon a herd of goats that crossed the road, with a stray dog following behind them. It wasn't unusual to see goats out here, but dogs didn't venture out onto the lava flow that encased the road between Aloha Village and the main highway. Jasmine collected stray dogs like Pua collected boyfriends. When she wasn't busy working at the resort, she volunteered at the Humane Society. She stopped the 4Runner and got out to see if she could catch the dog.

As she walked toward the stray, the dog trotted away and looked back periodically to keep her from coming any closer. It was skittish and would not come to her no matter how much she tried to coax it. Jasmine and the dog were headed right toward the bomb that Woo Ching had planted beside the road, under the cover of darkness, just before sunrise.

Woo Ching was nearby with binoculars and watched Jasmine and the stray head straight for the bomb. She wore a wide brim sun hat that morning that covered most of her face–he mistook her for Jessica.

His thumb hovered over the detonator button of the cell phone, as he waited until he was sure she was close enough to the bomb.

She continued to whistle and clap her hands together, as she tried to entice the skittish dog to come to her. Finally it stopped–a foot away from the bomb, that allowed her to grab his collar. Woo Ching watched through his binoculars–at the last second he saw it wasn't Jessica and set the detonator down.

As Woo Ching thought about blowing up Jasmine anyway, he saw a starburst-blue '69 Road Runner as it came up the road from Aloha Village. Jessica drove, as Sam sat in the passenger seat. The grin on Woo Ching's face said it all as he looked through the binoculars.

He grasped the cell phone detonator again and waited for all three of them to be in position before he triggered the bomb.

28

TOO CLOSE FOR COMFORT

Woo Ching had placed a small pile of white coral next to where he'd buried the bomb, to mark its location, so he could see it from the high ground on top of the cinder cone. What he didn't notice at the time, was there were other small piles of coral nearby. They marked a safe path to the beach, for four-wheel-drive vehicles, to keep them from falling into a lava tube, as they crossed over the flow.

Woo Ching clicked the dial button on the cell phone detonator, but the explosion he expected to kill the trio was at least a hundred feet away from them. The bomb was far enough away that Sam, Jessica, and Jasmine were out of the kill zone; the 4Runner was positioned at such an angle that it took the brunt of the force from the blast. The front windshield was blown out, and a lava rock two feet in diameter landed on the hood.

Just before the bomb exploded, Jasmine had run back down the road to where Sam and Jessica had stopped behind the 4Runner. She leaned in the window, and talked to them about the stray dog she had stopped for, when the bomb blast ripped through the morning calm.

"What the hell was that! Are you guys okay?" Sam said. Jasmine had been knocked down by the force of the blast. Jessica jumped out of the car to check on her.

"Are you okay, honey? Does it hurt anywhere?" Jessica could see the terror in her little sister's eyes and surveyed Jasmine for any visible shrapnel wounds, but she saw none.

"I'm okay," Jasmine said, as she sat up, dazed and bewildered.

Jessica scanned the surrounding area, and looked for any signs of the bomber. While Sam and Jasmine were still stunned, Jessica knew what had just happened. After two tours in Iraq with the National Guard, she'd seen her share of IEDs in-country and knew someone had just tried to kill them.

"The first thing we need to do is get off this road before something else bad happens," Jessica said. "Come on honey," Jessica said, as she reached for Jasmine's hand to get her back on her feet.

She helped Jasmine and the stray border collie into the backseat of the Road Runner. Sam sat shotgun, and they didn't waste any time getting back to the safety of Aloha Village.

When Woo Ching saw the bomb explode too far away from the targets, he heaved the cell phone detonator against a pile of rocks. He then hiked down the backside of the cinder cone to the beach and snuck back to the Ming to report the failed attempt to Mr. Lau.

WOO CHING EYES looked toward the floor as he said, "The bomb missed the target." There wasn't a trace of anger on Lau's face as he stood over the model of the proposed Ming expansion, moving pieces around the eight-foot-long table as he listened. Lau shifted his eyes toward the Triad's top assassin. "Since you failed, you should go back to Hong Kong, you seem to be incapable of handling a simple hit. I'll deal with this another way."

Woo Ching nodded and left the room. But he had aspirations of being in charge of the Triads, in the not-so-distant future, and could not return to Hong Kong until the job was complete. He had never failed to carry out an assignment, and this would not be the first time.

29

SECURITY

"Get cousin Keoki and tell him to stay with you at all times until I sort this out. Under no circumstance are you to leave the Village until you hear from me." As tears filled Jasmine's eyes, Jessica gave her a reassuring hug, as they stood outside the resort's office.

While Jessica got her sister situated, Sam ran to his bungalow, which was a short distance from the office, to get the satellite phone he kept for emergencies. He called Jim Davis, the captain of *The Ohana*.

"How far out are you from the island? There's been an incident here, and I need you to send a security team ASAP."

"About fifteen miles. How many men would you like me to send, sir?" Captain Davis asked.

"Send ten guys in the Sikorsky and have it land on the old airstrip behind the Village. At the same time, launch the tender and send it, too. I need it to take us to Honokohau Harbor. Have the team in khaki shorts and aloha shirts–tell them to keep the guns out of sight. I want them as low-profile as possible. They can use my bungalow as a command post. Continue on to Kailua Bay as planned and then set anchor there. I'll be staying on board *The Ohana* until this situation is under control."

Jim Davis had been the skipper of *The Ohana* a long time and had never heard such urgency in Sam's voice. Sam hired only retired Navy SEALs to provide shipboard security and seamanship on his superyacht. Actually, "superyacht" was an understatement. *The Ohana* was ninety-nine thousand tons and four hundred and fourteen feet long, with a crew of fifty-seven.

Sam walked at a brisk pace back toward the office where he met Jessica, who had waited out front for him. He watched as she tied up her hair into a messy bun. "I'm not sure if I'm having a hot flash or it's the humidity and all this excitement," she said, as she fanned herself.

"It smells like it's getting ready to rain, so it's probably not hormones. I couldn't deal with that right now, too." Sam nodded as he admired her hot, sweaty jungle look for a moment.

Not wanting to alert any of the Village's guests who were within earshot, coming and going into the office, she whispered, "We need to get to town, but we also need to not get killed on the way there."

Sam pulled the sat phone out of his pocket. "I have a plan. My tender will get here in about an hour, and we can take it to the Kailua Pier and get a taxi to the bank. Oh, by the way, I've taken the liberty of having some of my security force from my boat stay here and keep the Village safe."

Jessica studied Sam's face for a moment, thinking, *Who are you?* Her first thought was that she didn't need his help, but knew accepting it was the right thing to do.

She ignored her first thought and said, "That would be great, thank you." In the back of her mind was, *What tender is he talking about? How big is his "boat"?*

She had no choice but to let Sam help her. Self-reliant to a fault had always been a thing with her, ever since her mother had passed away, when she and her sisters were near adolescence. Since she was the oldest, her father had made her responsible for everything around the house.

Sam and Jessica walked down the beach toward the Ming to wait for the tender to arrive. There were a handful of guests that snorkeled in the bay and one guy that walked about twenty yards behind them, with a towel and a boom box that blasted an explicit rap song.

Jessica needed to call Uncle Jack and share the morning's assassination attempt with him, but first, she had to deal with a problem on the beach. And that problem's name was Grayson Roderick. Mr. Obnoxious—as Jasmine referred to him, had checked into the resort a week before and had quickly become a thorn in Jasmine's side with his constant complaints. But his intent today was to spread his unpleasantness and his loud music on the beach.

One of the selling points of Aloha Village, that differentiated it from all other resorts in Hawaii, was its "unplugged" policy—no electronics in the common areas or on the beach.

It was clear this guy didn't care about the rules. Jessica walked over to him where he had parked himself on the beach and asked him politely if he could turn down the music. She didn't even mention that he was breaking the rules. He glanced at her, and continued to talk on his cell phone as if she wasn't even there. She was in no mood for that nonsense. She picked up the ghetto blaster and hurled it into the bay before she walked back to where Sam sat on the beach.

As Mr. Obnoxious charged toward them, Sam jumped up and stepped in front of Jessica before the guy got within ten feet of her. He reached into his pocket for his wallet to offer to pay for the man's stereo. The buffoon answered with a fist that came toward Sam's face. Sam ducked and came back up with an uppercut that caught Roderick on the chin and knocked him out cold.

Sam liked to box to stay in shape almost as much as he liked to make money. "You should have taken the money," Sam said, as he pulled out his wallet and threw two hundred bucks at the guy lying in the sand. The bills landed next to the least favorite person on the beach. "This should cover your boom box."

When Roderick came to a few minutes later, Jasmine and cousin Keoki escorted him to his bungalow so he could pack–they'd enjoyed him all they could stand.

"We'll refund your money. You're out of here as soon as you pack. We've called you a taxi. Or we can call the cops and have you arrested for assault. Your choice," Jasmine said. As Roderick reached for his suitcase, she added, "Excellent choice."

Jessica didn't even skip a beat, she had been on her phone, and had left a message on Uncle Jack's answering machine, while Sam had defended her. It'd been years since a man had taken up for her. Chivalry wasn't dead and a girl could get used to that. Little did Sam know, she didn't need him to defend her, but she liked that he had.

30

UNCLE JACK HUI HOU

Uncle Jack was in the head of the *Hui Hou* when he heard Jessica leave a message on his answering machine. "Someone just tried to blow us up with an IED on the road leaving the Village."

He grumbled something to himself about never eating spicy Thai food again as he dialed Jessica's phone number.

"Where are you now?"

"Sitting on the beach at the Village, waiting for Sam's tender to pick us up–it's too dangerous to drive to town."

"Stop by. We need to talk."

"That's why I'm calling. I have a check to deposit that will save the Village, and I need to borrow your Bronco."

"Okay, I'll have it waiting for you. Do you have a weapon with you?"

"No, all my guns are still in the shipping container."

"I'll have a nine-millimeter ready for you, too."

"Thanks." And Jessica clicked off her cell phone.

After he'd gotten off the phone with Jessica Uncle Jack didn't waste any time dialing Jin Tanaka.

Jin didn't recognize Uncle Jack's phone number and let it go to voicemail.

"Jin, we have a problem." Uncle Jack proceeded to leave a message that detailed what had just happened to Jessica, Sam, and Jasmine. Uncle Jack couldn't protect his nieces, but he knew the yakuza would–they were family.

TWENTY MINUTES before the tender arrived at Aloha Village, the Sikorsky helicopter landed and dropped off the security force to secure the Village. Sam took the team leader around and introduced him to Jasmine, cousin Keoki and other key employees of the small resort before he went back to the beach to wait for the tender to arrive.

Sam reassured Jessica that his guys would keep a low profile and they'd blend in so as not to alarm the guests. She knew there was safety in numbers, and she felt safe with Sam. Soon, they spotted the tender as it came into the bay in front of the resort. Technically, it was called a tender, but in most circles, people would call it a small yacht.

Jessica stared at the two-tone white and dark blue boat as is drifted in toward the beach. "About sixty feet?" she asked.

"Good guess, sixty-five," Sam replied.

"Aloha, Mr. Stewart," yelled Terry Barnes, the coxswain, as he drifted the big boat up as close to the beach in front of Aloha Village as he could get without getting stuck in the shallows. Sam and Jessica waded out, and Terry helped them both aboard from the rear swim deck.

"Good to see you again, Mr. Stewart," Terry said.

"As it is you, Mr. Barnes," Sam answered as he shook Terry's hand.

Sam placed his hand on the small of Jessica's back. "This is Jessica Kealoha."

"It's a pleasure to meet you, Ms. Kealoha."

"Aloha, Terry. You can call me Jessica."

"Honey, if you go down below to the saloon, you can

make yourself comfortable. I'll be down there in a minute," Sam said.

Jessica gave Sam a devilish look as she stepped through the sliding glass door to enter the saloon. *It's good to have someone who calls you honey,* she thought.

As she headed for the saloon, Sam gave Terry instructions to take them to the *Hui Hou*'s slip at the harbor.

31

GOLF PRO

Jin listened to Jack Murphy's message, while on his way to eat dinner with his ninety-four-year-old father, Eizō. They met every week to talk about yakuza business. His father was the original yakuza boss who had started the gang in Hawaii. The meeting always took place at a little out-of-the-way diner in downtown Honolulu that had the best saimin in town.

Though Jin was the boss of the yakuza in Hawaii, Eizō insisted he call Lance Ishikawa in Kona, the yakuza's enforcer on the Big Island. For the most part, the yakuza had a strict hands-off policy regarding the outer islands, except for a few nefarious activities here and there. This was family the Triads had messed with, and now it was time to send them a message. A dead body should get their attention.

Mr. Lau was going to host a critical golf tournament at the Ming and had sent his chauffeur to meet the plane of Zhang Wei, a golf pro from Shanghai that Mr. Lau had personally invited to play in the tournament. Mr. Wei was a very famous and influential golfer in China and could send a lot of business to the Ming, if he liked the resort and its golf course.

Lance Ishikawa parked alongside the road which exited the Ming, propped open the hood of his Sprinter van to make it look like he had engine trouble. The vehicle looked like any of the island tour vans that came and went from the Ming–except it wasn't. It was a yakuza murder wagon in disguise. Inside were all the tools necessary to dispose of a body without leaving a trace. Jin had taught Lance that the best way to get rid of a body was to put it in a fifty-five-gallon drum, fill it with concrete, and dump it at sea. If there was no body, then there was no evidence and would be no conviction. This time was different, they would send the body back to the Ming to make a point. It was risky from a prosecution standpoint, but necessary. There would be no mistaking the message they had sent the Triads.

When the Ming's limousine passed by Lance, he closed the hood, hopped in the Sprinter and followed the car to the Kona airport. The limo had parked in the cell phone lot, to wait for the golfer's plane to land. Lance parked next to the limo and watched the driver for a few minutes before he made his move. The chauffeur was still looking down at his phone when Ishikawa walked up to the driver's side window and reached in with a stun gun. He stuck it to the chauffeur's neck and pulled the trigger, yanked him out of the limo, opened the side door of the van and threw him on the floor.

After he'd gagged and zip tied the driver, he grabbed the man's cell phone as he got in the limo, and waited for the call to pick up the golf pro at the curb. Thirty minutes later the limo driver's cell phone rang and Ishikawa left the cell phone lot to pick up Zhang Wei, less than five minutes later he was in the back of the limo and headed toward certain death.

Ishikawa drove to the southernmost part of the airport, past where all the private jets parked, and pulled the limo over. Zhang Wei was in the back of the car as he talked on his cell phone and didn't notice what was going on. Ishikawa walked to the rear passenger side door as he obscured an ice pick. He flung the door open and stabbed Zhang Wei in the chest before he had time to react. Zhang Wei was dead seconds after the pick perforated his heart.

Ishikawa took the limo back to the cell phone lot and drugged the chauffeur before he put him back in the limo. He returned to the Sprinter and drove out of the parking lot just like any of the other commercial vehicles that came and went that day.

MR. LAU HAD BEEN in his office talking on the phone with Governor Fitch about what to do concerning Aloha Village when his secretary burst into the room and handed him a bloody note.

A message had been pinned to Zhang Wei's chest that said, "Next time it's your wife. Then it will be you. The best thing you can do is get back on your private jet and go back to Hong Kong where you came from."

It was evident to Lau that someone connected to Jessica Kealoha had murdered Zhang Wei. He'd made a dangerous enemy when he ordered Woo Ching to kill her. What Lau didn't know was that Jessica's uncle and grandfather were the leaders of the Japanese mob in Hawaii, and they had no qualms about killing anyone who threatened their family. The yakuza owned Hawaii, and the Triads had not only tried to kill Jessica, but as the yakuza saw it, they were trespassing and would be punished for it.

There were no secrets on the Big Island, and it didn't take long for Lau to find out that Jessica was connected to the yakuza–by blood. Even though she was a retired cop, the yakuza would protect her because she was family. Lau knew he had made a formidable enemy now and would have to deal with it. The first thing he did was to call Woo Ching. He knew Woo Ching had not left the island yet, and he would need him for personal security until this situation with Jessica and the yakuza was resolved.

"There's a change in plans. I need you to finish the job."

"What do you want me to do?" Woo Ching asked.

"I still need Jessica Kealoha dead."

Woo Ching smiled as he listened to his uncle. This time he wouldn't fail.

Even though Lau was a relative newcomer to the island, and was there to build a mega gambling resort once gambling became legal, he was Chinese. And they had roots on the island going back to the 1800s, just like the Japanese. As in World War Two, they would fight it out again, but this time it would be a gang war between the two sides. The Triads had about twenty members in Kona, and Lau thought they could handle the yakuza, who he knew had little presence on the Big Island. What he didn't realize–that was about to change.

THE NEXT DAY Eizō and Jin met again at lunch time in the small diner to plan the next step to kick the Triads out of Hawaii.

Eizō asked Jin, "Lance sent the message?"

"Yes."

"Good."

Eizō stared down into his bowl as he stirred the noodles of saimin, then looked up at Jin. "The Triads are tough. Don't underestimate them. They won't go until we make it too uncomfortable for them to stay. And if they've decided Jessica must die, they won't stop until she is dead, or we've convinced them otherwise."

Jin nodded, stirred soy sauce into a small dab of wasabi. "Or until we kill every last one of them."

Eizō nodded with a slight smile. "Jin, I know you and Jessica have had differences in the past. But she's still my granddaughter. The cops can't protect her. It's up to us."

Even though Eizō had retired and handed the day-to-day operations of the yakuza over to Jin years before, Eizō still had the final say about anything related to yakuza business in Hawaii. Jin never questioned the orders of his father, who spent most of his days tending to his prize-winning koi.

"Get the men together and go to Kona. The Triads won't go without a fight," Eizō said, as he slid his bowl of saimin away with a look of disgust on his face.

"*Hai!*" Jin answered.

The yakuza had a fleet of fishing boats they operated out of Oahu. Jin sent the biggest one of them which had a crew of twenty-three men. That was all he would need to teach the Triads a lesson.

32

UNCLE JACK

Sam's tender dropped him and Jessica off at the fuel dock at Honokohau Harbor. They walked over to the *A Hui Hou*'s slip to borrow Uncle Jack's truck.

When they arrived at the slip, Uncle Jack sat in the fighting chair, nursed a beer while he read *Fish News* and puffed on a cigar.

When he saw them he put the cigar out and got up, grabbed a small backpack out of the saloon he'd gotten ready for Jessica earlier. He brought it out to the cockpit and set it in the fighting chair.

"You guys look good for people who almost got blown up today." Uncle Jack smiled.

"Nothing like a bomb first thing in the morning to get your day started off right," Sam joked. Jessica cut her eyes toward him. It was apparent she didn't see the humor in it.

Uncle Jack picked his cigar back up, relit it and took a drag. "After you called me, I thought about how the bomb was made and came to the conclusion it had to have been assembled using chemicals bought without suspicion." Jessica nodded. She knew where he was going with this, and Sam did too. Although he wasn't in law enforcement, he was a smart guy, and his first thought had been of the Oklahoma City bombing–a fertilizer bomb.

Uncle Jack handed Jessica a surveillance photo of Woo Ching. She knew the next step to take after going to the bank to deposit the check from Auntie Loana. A trip to the farm supply store to see if anyone who worked there recognized the man in the photo.

"There's a Smith & Wesson Slim Nine in the bag and ten paper targets to keep the cops from arresting you for concealed carry. Just remember, you're on the way to target practice." Uncle Jack winked.

Smiling at Uncle Jack, Jessica grabbed the bag with one hand and held out her other.

"Oops, sorry. Here's the keys to my old Ford. You can't miss it. It's parked over there." Uncle Jack pointed east toward the parking lot in front of the Fishing Club building, about a hundred yards from the *Hui Hou*.

Uncle Jack had a blue-and-white '67 Ford Bronco with a 351 Cleveland engine. Jessica was always excited to drive her dad and Uncle Jack's vehicles because they both always had to drive something that was fast. She figured they were both a couple of adrenaline junkies that got off on going a hundred and thirty miles an hour down the Queen K when nobody was around. Just thinking about it produced a warm memory of how her dad would take her to the Hilo drag strip and let her race his Road Runner when she was sixteen. By the time she had turned seventeen, she was a feared bracket racer at the track, she regularly proved that women had faster reflexes than men. All things being equal, she would win nine times out of ten.

Uncle Jack's Bronco looked like an old piece of crap, just the way he liked it. He never had to worry about anybody banging into it in a parking lot. Even though the paint job was faded and it had primer grey that covered the previous rust spots, it was in fair condition from outward appearances. In street racer jargon, it was a sleeper. Under the hood was a custom-built street/strip dyno-tuned engine that put out an easy five hundred horsepower to the ground which made it down right exciting when the gas pedal was mashed to the floor.

Sam strapped in, as he sat shotgun, as Jessica fired up the big Ford engine and pointed the rocket, disguised as a Bronco, toward the bank in town so they could deposit the check that would save Aloha Village.

THE DRIVE into town was uneventful and after she deposited Auntie Loana's check, for one point two million dollars, Jessica called Jasmine to let her know Aloha Village could pay bills without worry now. And that she and Sam were on their way to try and find out who'd tried to kill them earlier that day.

When they walked into the farm supply store and showed the photo of Woo Ching to the young man who worked that day, the clerk remembered he'd seen him in the store because he had been wearing a suit. At the time, the clerk had thought it was strange a guy in a suit wanted to buy fertilizer.

Sam and Jessica thanked the clerk and headed back to the harbor to return Uncle Jack's Bronco.

Sam asked Jessica. "What do you think?"

"Let's find Woo Ching and hope he forces me to put a bullet in him."

Sam's eyes grew big.

Then she laughed. "I'm just kidding. Sort of. Okay, not," she said with a passive aggressive tone.

"How about we go talk to the Kona PD instead, before going back to the harbor?" Sam suggested.

"If we were on the mainland, that would be the right way to handle this. But the thing that scares me is that talking to the police here might be the same as discussing it with Mr. Lau himself because of spies in the department."

She thought about it for a moment. "Let's go see my old partner, Sid Akiona, I heard a while back he still works there. He's the only one I would trust."

"Why do you think the department has spies?" Sam asked.

"Most of the cops working there are somebody's cousin– here on the island. That's why we have to be very careful about who we talk to."

Sam nodded.

Jessica continued to talk as she drove toward the police station,

"When I started out in law enforcement, I got hired by the Kona PD after graduating from the police academy. And like I said, Sid was my training officer. He was a standup guy. When the department accused me of theft, as a young rookie, Sid was the only one who'd stood up for me. He knew for a fact I didn't steal the missing fifty thousand dollars out of the police evidence room. At the time, it was still an old boys' club and women had not been welcome in the department. Any way they could get rid of a woman was okay with most of the upper echelon, and I was no exception. Everyone knew the theft allegation was a ruse. But I had made a powerful enemy when I wrote the chief of police a ticket for being parked in a red zone at a local hotel, where he was having a nooner with his mistress. Even the internal affairs detectives, who investigated the missing money, knew I didn't do it. But I was being blamed by a senior officer who was the brother-in-law of the chief. There was talk around the station that one of the evidence room workers had stolen the money, but they never filed charges and I was the scapegoat they'd tried to pin it on. I had allegedly been the last one in the room before the theft was discovered. I was cleared six months after the investigation. But it was obvious to me that the stink of the accusation would never go away. That was when I quit and moved to LA, so I could go to work for a big-city department where nepotism isn't allowed."

Jessica had a mixture of butterflies and hostility in her gut as she turned the Bronco off of the highway just a half a block a way from the station.

33

KONA PD

Jessica parked the Bronco far enough away from the entrance to the police station so that nobody, inside the building, would see what she and Sam were doing while seated inside the vehicle. Uncle Jack had a custom-built gun safe installed into the floor of the Bronco; Jessica put the Smith & Wesson Slim Nine inside it and locked the door. No need to test out Uncle's target practice excuse story, she thought.

Sam and Jessica walked through the front, double glass doors and up to the desk sergeant. "Is Officer Sid Akiona on shift today?" Jessica asked the young policeman behind the counter.

"Yes, the watch commander is in his office, I believe. Let me see for sure. Who should I tell him is here to see him?"

"Tell him Jessica Kealoha."

A few minutes later, the young policeman returned with Sid Akiona, who was now Captain Akiona. Sid's face lit up with a welcoming smile when he saw Jessica. He was genuinely glad to see her. It had been close to twenty years since the last time they had seen each other. After a warm embrace, Jessica introduced Sam. He shook the captain's hand, though he wasn't crazy about the way the captain looked at Jessica, like they had once been more than just coworkers. It was a weird feeling Sam couldn't seem to shake while they were talking.

"I heard about your father, Jessica. I'm so sorry for your loss," Akiona said.

"Thank you. The reason we're here today is that someone tried to blow us up two days ago, with a roadside bomb planted near the exit of Aloha Village. It exploded about sixty yards from us. We were lucky no one was injured."

Captain Akiona's face was expressionless as Sam and Jessica recounted the harrowing details of how they'd almost lost their lives and how they suspected Woo Ching.

Jessica also mentioned that she and Sam had gone to the farm supply store to see if Woo Ching had been there to buy fertilizer; they suspected it was the main ingredient used to make the bomb. And that they found a clerk who positively identified Woo Ching, from a photo they showed him, as having purchased a bag of fertilizer.

Akiona looked puzzled and then asked, "Where did you get the photo of the guy?"

"My uncle, Jack Murphy."

"You think this Woo Ching is responsible?"

Jessica nodded. "If it's not him, then it was probably Mother Teresa."

"I see you haven't lost your keen sense of humor. We'll start looking for this guy, and if we find him, we'll bring him in for a chat and see if we can make a case."

Sam and Jessica both shook the captain's hand and thanked him for his time. Sam then asked one last question before they left.

"What's the chances of getting a concealed carry permit these days?"

Jessica already knew the answer but stood by patiently, knowing what the reply would be.

Captain Akiona shook his head. "The chief won't issue them. Never has and said he never will."

"Even if we're in danger?" Sam asked.

"The chief is adamant about not having civilians walking around carrying guns."

"Interesting." Sam shook his head in disbelief.

Jessica smiled and thanked the captain again for his time, then grabbed Sam's hand and steered him toward the door.

As Sam and Jessica drove out of the police station parking lot, Sam looked at Jessica. "Maybe I'm wrong, but I felt an underlying tension between you and Captain Akiona back there. Did you and the good captain have something going on once upon a time?"

Jessica steered the Bronco onto the Queen K Highway to head back toward the harbor. Sam reached down to unlock the gun safe, as he waited for her to answer. She kept her eyes on the road and finally answered, "Let's just say that when we were partners on the night shift–he wanted to be naked partners, too. But I wasn't interested." She placed her right hand on Sam's thigh.

Sam felt jealous as he thought about another man wanting Jessica. But her hand on his thigh made the jealous feelings fade away.

Sam's phone buzzed in his pocket, and he looked down to see who the text was from.

"Why don't we stay on my boat until this is over? I got a text that *The Ohana* has arrived and is anchored in Kailua Bay."

Jessica didn't hesitate. "I can't leave Jasmine alone. I know she's safe with your guys there in the Village, but I have to go back to the resort until this is over."

Sam sighed, but he understood where she was coming

from. "Okay, back to the Village we go. I'll call the tender to pick us up at the harbor after we return the Bronco."

Jessica looked at Sam and smiled. "Since your guys have taken over your bungalow, you'll have to stay with me–at mine."

Sam grinned. "Well, if you insist." And they both laughed.

34

SASHIMI MARU

The *Sashimi Maru* had trolled the Kona coast for the past few days. It appeared to be a Japanese fishing boat like any other. Except what wasn't obvious it belonged to the yakuza. It was the largest tuna boat they ran out of Oahu, and besides catching fish, it was a tool used to launder money. And now its crew plotted their attack on the Triads. With a crew of twenty-three, they had no fear of the Triads outnumbering them.

Their plan was simple: go ashore at night and burn Lau's villa to the ground while he slept. The worst-case scenario was that he survived the fire. But the fire should be enough to convince him, if he managed to survive, that staying in Kona would be hazardous to his health if he managed to survive, and he should go back to China. The best-case scenario was that he died in the fire, and the Triads in Hong Kong would know Hawaii was enemy territory. There would be an understanding that if they ever came back, they'd would pay with their lives.

It was about 3:30 a.m. when Jin Tanaka sent ten men ashore in the *Sashimi Maru*'s motor launch. They had ten five-gallon gas cans and a box of flares. The yakuza didn't blow things up. They specialized in extortion, prostitution and smuggling guns from Hawaii to Japan. Burning down Lau's villa at the Ming was not something they would do without serious provocation, but the Triads had attempted to kill two of the granddaughters of Eizō Tanaka. The yakuza would make them pay the price for their transgression.

Jin Tanaka told his guys where to find Lau's villa on the grounds and made it clear that they weren't to burn any part of the Ming where guests stayed. The yakuza would kill when they had to, but killing innocent people like tourists was not good for business and would bring the feds in force. Killing the leader of the Triads in Hawaii would most likely only bring a local response, and it would be lukewarm at best. Tanaka had men on the payroll throughout the state government, including the Kona PD, and would be able to control the investigation, as he had in the past.

By 4:15 a.m., Jin Tanaka could see the glow of Lau's villa engulfed in flames. Jin smoked a cigarette topside of the *Sashimi Maru* while he watched the villa burn to the ground through his binoculars. *"Good riddance,"* he said.

As the group of Japanese thugs headed back toward the motor launch at the beach, they came across a wild goat that had been munching grass on the golf course. They killed it and threw it in the resort's swimming pool as a message to the Triads that they'd best plan to leave Hawaii.

When the fire department arrived on scene at the Ming, Lau's villa was destroyed. There was nothing left to save. But Tanaka didn't know Lau wasn't there. He had stayed in one of the resort's guest rooms because he feared retaliation from the yakuza–and rightly so.

❦

THE YAKUZA HAD a spy who worked at the Ming that Tanaka had been checking in with, during his visits to take Kainoa to the beach. Jin liked taking Kainoa to the beach, but his weekly visits to the Big Island were about a lot more than just being a good uncle. Figuring out what the Triads were up to had been his number one goal for the past six months. China White fentanyl was what they were up to, besides trying to get gambling legalized and take over Aloha Village.

The yakuza had known the Triads had been shipping fentanyl to the Big Island and hadn't cared–until now. They had been planning to rip off the drugs for some time and decided this would be the perfect time to kill two birds with one stone. Lance Ishikawa waited with the murder wagon to take five of the ten men, sent ashore, to the Triads' body shop to steal the drugs while the other five burned down Mr. Lau's villa at the Ming.

Jin Tanaka's inside man at the Ming frequently saw exotic high-end European cars being shipped to the resort in a container from Hong Kong every month. Jin figured the Triads hid drugs in the vehicles; sending them in containers made it almost impossible for drug-sniffing dogs to catch them.

Once the car arrived, Mr. Lau would have Woo Ching take the vehicle to a body shop the Triads owned, in the old industrial area, to have it dismantled and painted. Afterward, the cars would be shipped to the mainland and sold at auction. Financially, it made little sense. The vehicles cost more in Hong Kong than they did in the US, and it cost more to ship them to Hawaii—unless they were carried two or three kilos of China White hidden inside them.

Tanaka had no desire to go into the business of selling dope. Hookers, guns, and extortion were okay, but drugs were taboo to the yakuza. The way he saw it, this was free money. He would dump the fentanyl at a discount to move it fast and donate some of the proceeds to a drug rehab center on the island.

35

LANAI

Sam and Jessica sat on the lanai, having their morning coffee, when Jessica's phone rang. She looked at the screen to see who was calling so early and saw it was Uncle Jack and knew it would be important.

"Just a heads-up—the cops will come to see you soon."

"Why?"

"They got called to the Ming a few days ago about a dead Chinese golfer. He was found in the back of their limousine at the airport, deader than a door nail. They think it was a professional hit, from the intelligence I've got. The limo driver told the cops a wild story about being abducted and then waking up back in the limousine later with the dead guy in the backseat. My source says at first the cops weren't buying it, but then there was a witness who corroborated his story, saying he saw the limo driver get stuffed back into the car from a van that parked right next to it."

"Why does the Kona PD want to talk to me?"

"My source says Lau told them you would do anything to disrupt his business and might somehow be connected to the murder and burning down his villa."

Jessica's forehead wrinkled. "Figures. Thanks for the heads-up."

"I guess he thinks if he can't kill you, he'll try to get you locked up. Oh, one last thing. Be careful."

"Something I ought to know?" Jessica asked.

"That's all I can say right now." Uncle Jack was quick to hang up the phone.

I hate it when he pulls that secret agent crap on me, she thought. After she sat the phone down she caught a glimpse of something moving under the table near her foot. She jumped up from her chair and stomped on a centipede a half a dozen times to make sure it was dead. It had slithered out of a hole between the rocks in the staircase that led to the lanai.

Sam couldn't see what had prompted her to jump up because the table was between the two of them and blocked his view of the prehistoric-looking creature that was approximately six inches long and had what looked like a thousand legs.

"Take that," Jessica said as she ground what remained of the centipede's head into the wood flooring of the lanai.

Sam peered over the edge of the table.

"Yup, you killed the crap out of him." And they both laughed.

"Literally," she replied.

"Feel better?"

"Yes, I do."

WHEN DETECTIVE GOMES showed up at Aloha Village, Sam and Jessica were on stand-up paddle boards in the middle of the bay fronting the resort. Jessica had been trying to lose the ten pounds she'd gained.

That was the thing about being back in Hawaii—potato

mac and two scoops of rice always came with the plate lunch, and a zillion carbs to boot. Until her thirties, she could eat anything and not gain an ounce. After forty, just looking at a chocolate cake seemed to equal gaining five pounds. The last couple of weeks since her father's death, she'd been hitting the chocolate cake hard.

Coffee, booze, cigarettes, and donuts used to be Jessica's four major food groups; now she was just down to sugar. It was a reasonable compromise in her mind. Besides, unlike booze, nobody ever got arrested for eating cake.

Detective Gomes never met a malasada he didn't like. He sat down at the Castaway Bar, that overlooked the bay, and helped himself to a box of the tasty Portuguese treats the resort had put out that morning for guests. He ate the whole box while he waited for Sam and Jessica to paddle back in. At three hundred and thirty pounds, and gaining, Gomes's motto was "Eat until you're tired, not until you're full."

Jessica didn't recognize Gomes from her early days on the force, but he remembered her, and the allegations made against her years earlier. He didn't care one way or the other about Jessica being a dirty cop, but he doubted she'd had anything to do with the murder of the golf pro.

"Ms. Kealoha, if you have a few minutes, I'd like a word." He introduced himself and handed her his card. She glanced at his name on it.

"How can I help you, Detective Gomes?"

"Can you account for your whereabouts the day before yesterday?"

Sam interjected, "She was with me."

"And you are?" Gomes asked.

"I'm Sam Stewart. We were here all day, lying on the beach and snorkeling. Plenty of the staff here at the resort saw us."

Gomes looked down at his notebook and nodded as he wrote down Sam's name.

"I think this should do it," Gomes said. And that was it. He grabbed one more malasada, from a new box on the bar, and ate it on the way back to his car. Sam and Jessica never heard another word from him.

36

KIDNAPPED

The Kona PD had looked for Woo Ching for nearly a week and had come up empty. Jessica was tired of waiting. It would be up to her and Sam to bring him to justice.

Jessica was sure they had a spy at Aloha Village who fed info to Lau. How else would the Triads have known she was on her way to the bank to deposit a check, to save the Village, the day Woo Ching tried to kill them? It was clear someone had tipped them off and Jessica decided she would use the mole to set a trap for Woo Ching. What she and Sam didn't know was that Woo Ching had set a trap of his own–that would preempt their plan.

❦

BESIDES WORKING part-time for her dad at the Village, Jasmine was a massage therapist. She had a side business at the resort that she had operated the past couple of years, so she could raise money to go to college to become a veterinarian.

She was a busy girl. That was the thing about Mike

Murphy's daughters—they were all hard workers and always tried to get ahead financially.

Jasmine was in her office doing paperwork when her cell phone rang. "Aloha, this is Jasmine."

"Howzit, I got your name from a friend who highly recommended you for a massage, would this afternoon would be good if you have the time," the man said.

She looked at her calendar for a moment, it was going to be tough to fit him in, but she needed the money and said, "How about two o'clock? If that works for you, meet me at the cabana on the beach here at Aloha Village."

"That's perfect," the man replied.

Between the resort's guests, and word of mouth, Jasmine didn't need to advertise for business. But she always asked who had referred the new client so she could send them a thank-you card for the referral.

Woo Ching had used a common Japanese surname when Jasmine had asked him who referred him. She had two clients with that same name and thought she would figure out which one it was when she met her new client at two p.m.

Sam's security team had a photo of Woo Ching and had been warned to be on the lookout for him. But unknown to anyone–Woo Ching was a master of disguise. He put on a wig and a fake beard, and when he showed up for the two o'clock massage, he looked like a harmless old man. Nobody recognized him, and he had booked under a phony name. He knew Sam's security team was in the Village and that he would have to trick Jasmine into walking him to his car in the parking lot, where he would drug and abduct her.

As Jasmine kneaded the muscles in her new client's neck she said,

"It was great timing when you called, I had a last-minute cancellation that opened up a slot for you. Otherwise, I would have been short of money for my veterinarian school tuition on the mainland that I'm saving for."

Woo Ching tuned in on that as the weakness he would exploit to get her to walk out to his car.

"You're going to be an animal doctor? You should come look at my poi dog puppy I just got, he's in the car and something's not right with him. Since you love animals, maybe you can tell me what's wrong with him."

Jasmine had been volunteering at the animal clinic in town for the last year and had learned a lot, so she thought it wouldn't hurt to look at his dog and possibly recommend he bring it in to the animal hospital she worked at.

After the massage, Jasmine and what appeared to be an old man strolled to the parking lot arm in arm, and when security offered to escort them, she waved them off. "No need."

HOURS LATER, Jasmine woke up groggy and with a headache from the drug-induced state she had been in. She laid on a concrete floor in the fetal position in a room that was only eight feet wide by eight feet long, with plywood walls and a low plywood ceiling. The roof wasn't even high enough to allow her to stand up inside the box. Woo Ching had padlocked her inside the makeshift prison at a warehouse in the old industrial area. The only thing she remembered was leaning in the window of the old man's car to look at the dog. As soon as she'd leaned in, Woo Ching had pulled a rag, soaked in chloroform, out of his pocket and smothered her face with it.

The warehouse belonged to Lau. It was in a row of them he owned, located at the very end of the road behind a locked gate.

Jasmine screamed for help for hours, but it wasn't coming. Woo Ching had set up a camera in the room and kept her under surveillance with an app on his phone that had a two-way speaker built-in.

"You're wasting your time. No one can hear you. You're inside a building that is soundproof, and there is no one around," the voice said to Jasmine through a speaker mounted on the ceiling of the box, in which she was being held prisoner.

"Who are you? What do you want? Please, let me out of here," she cried.

"I want your sister. And you're the bait," the voice answered.

Jasmine quit crying. "You know she'll kill you for this, right?"

There was no reply from the voice on the other end of the speaker.

Woo Ching had taken Jasmine's phone when she was unconscious and found Jessica's phone number in it, he then had thrown the phone out the window on the way to the warehouse. He knew Jessica would check the phone records to see the cell tower location of the last ping from Jasmine's phone to get an idea where she might be.

THE NEXT DAY, Woo Ching called Jessica from a burner phone, but since she didn't recognize the number, she let it go to voicemail.

Momi was the front desk clerk at Aloha Village that day and when the phone rang, she answered it like she always had. "Aloha, this is–." The man on the other end of the line interrupted her, "Shut up and listen. You tell Jessica Kealoha I'm holding Jasmine and if she doesn't follow my directions I'm going to kill her little sister."

The man's voice sent shivers down Momi's spine as she

listened to what he said. "Okay, okay, I'll tell her. Please don't hurt Jasmine!" Momi cried.

Minutes later she called Jessica, "Slow down Momi, take a breath, I can barely understand you," Jessica said. As Momi cried, she repeated exactly what the man said.

"He said to tell you to check your voicemail, and if you ever want to see her again, you better answer your phone the next time he calls." Jessica felt a pang of fear in her gut as she asked Momi about Jasmine's schedule before she'd disappeared.

"She had a massage client yesterday at two p.m., and nobody has seen her since that time. But she had a college class afterward, so no one thought anything about it," Momi said.

Sam sat on the lanai, and worked on a proposal for the Hawaii ferry, when he heard Jessica on the phone inside the bungalow. He could tell from her side of the conversation, and the tone of her voice, that something was very wrong. After Jessica hung up, he set his laptop down on the table, went inside and asked her, "What happened?"

"Jasmine has been kidnapped! I'm going to go find the man responsible for this."

"We," Sam interjected.

"Okay, we have to go look for her." Jessica grabbed her thigh holster off the kitchen counter and slipped it over her right leg under her sundress, then stuffed the nine-millimeter pistol in it that Uncle Jack had loaned her.

In LA, she always wore jeans and carried a backup gun in an ankle holster at work. She almost felt naked without it and mumbled something to that effect, and Sam heard it.

"Not a problem. I'll be back in a few minutes." Sam went to his bungalow, where his security team had set up shop, and returned with two Glock 19s and a couple of extra magazines of ammo. "This should be enough, don't you think?" He handed Jessica one of the Glocks and an extra clip with fifteen rounds in it.

She grabbed her small backpack, put the gun inside, slung it over her shoulder and said, "Let's go."

Jessica fired up the 426 Hemi engine in her father's '69 Road Runner and backed it out of the garage. She then got out of the car while the engine warmed up, which was necessary for that cold-blooded beast. The look on her face worried Sam.

"This is too dangerous," she said. "You don't need to come with me. Besides, if something happened to you, I wouldn't be able to cope with it again."

"Again?" Sam asked.

"My first husband and I were on a stakeout one night," Jessica started, and then her phone rang.

"This is Jessica Kealoha," she answered quickly.

"Your sister will die if you don't do what I tell you," the voice on the other end said in broken English.

"Okay, what do you want?"

Sam could tell the rumble of the big Hemi engine was making it hard to hear, so he shut it down while Jessica was on the phone.

"We want our merchandise back," the caller said.

"I don't understand what the hell you're talking about."

"The yakuza ripped us off–is what I'm talking about."

It became crystal-clear to Jessica right at that moment what had happened. She needed no further explanation.

"If I can get your drugs back, you'll let my sister go?"

"That's the deal, lady. There will be a cigarette boat at VV buoy at six p.m tonight. Show up with our ten kilos, and we'll release your sister after the drop. If you bring Five-O with you, your sister is dead." And the phone went dead.

Jessica had put Woo Ching on speaker so Sam could hear the whole conversation. She was mentally tough, but this was almost too much. Sam could see her eyes well up with tears as she walked back inside the bungalow.

"If we call the FBI, they could—"

She cut him off and held up her hand. "We're not. I know who to call. The only way this works out is if the Triads get their drugs back."

Sam thought better of arguing with her. Besides, she was more of an expert at this sort of thing than him. All he knew was how to build superyachts. Jessica was the expert at dealing with criminals. But Sam was an expert when it came to risk assessment. And this situation looked as risky as swimming with sharks to him.

For the first time in three years, Jessica wanted to pour herself a gin and tonic and think about the whole thing. But that choice was no longer available to her, so she did the next best thing. She went to the bathroom, so Sam couldn't hear, and called her grandfather, Eizō Tanaka, over in Honolulu.

"Hi, Grandpa. It's Jessica. Jasmine has been taken hostage by the Triads. They want their dope back or they'll kill her."

"I'll make a phone call," Eizō said, and he hung up the phone.

Jessica walked back into the living room and sat down on the couch, she exhaled a guarded sigh of relief.

Sam sat next to her and rested his hand on her leg. "Why don't you want to call the FBI? I don't get it. We're talking about Jasmine's life and stolen drugs, and you don't want their help. What am I missing here?"

"There's not enough time. The nearest office is in Honolulu, by the time they get here, it'll be too late. There won't be enough agents, and the Triads will kill Jasmine before the FBI has a game plan. The other reason is my family. I guess now is as good a time as any to bring out the skeletons. You'll probably never want to see me again after you hear this."

Sam stared at Jessica as she stood up and paced back and

forth in the living room for a minute, before she said another word.

"I know who has the Triads' dope. It's one of my uncles on my mother's side of the family." And then she paused for a moment. "Three of my uncles on my mother's side are yakuza gang members. My grandfather on my mother's side is the founder of the yakuza in Hawaii."

Sam said nothing and just listened as Jessica shared one of her deepest, darkest secrets. The shame was written all over her face.

He stood up from the couch and walked over to Jessica, and wrapped his arms around her. "I've got skeletons too," he whispered in her ear.

IT HAD BEEN six hours since Jessica had called her grandfather, and she had heard nothing. She and Sam sat at the dining room table and cleaned their guns to pass the time, while they waited to find out where the Triads' stolen drugs were.

From where Jessica sat she had a view straight out the window and saw Pua's Mercedes as it drove up the driveway. Pua had come to the bungalow to get Sam's signature on closing documents for the house he'd bought in Keauhou. She had been worked hard the last month, to get the deal closed, and thought the day would be one of celebration instead of the bad news about Jasmine that she got.

After Pua got out of her Mercedes and walked up the steps to the lanai, she could see the grim expressions on both Sam and Jessica's faces through the dining room window.

"Did someone die, or is someone going to?" Pua said in a half-kidding tone of voice, as she eyeballed both of them focused on the guns–and not her.

Jessica continued to polish the barrel of the Glock, and

didn't make eye contact. "Jasmine's missing. She's been gone about eighteen hours or so."

Pua threw the papers in her hand down on the kitchen table and glared at her older sister. "When did you plan on telling me?"

Jessica had been hoping not to have to tell her until after they had rescued Jasmine. She knew Pua had enough on her plate with having breast cancer and didn't need any additional stress.

"I'm sorry. I was hoping to have her back home before you found out."

"Why are you sitting here and not out trying to get her back?"

Jessica stuck the Glock 19 in her ankle holster. "We're waiting for Uncle Jin to call and tell us where we can find the ransom so we can exchange it for Jasmine."

"How much do they want?" Pua asked.

"It's not money they want. And the less you know about it, the better," Jessica said.

Pua had done enough shady real estate deals over the years to know when to quit asking questions, and she recognized this was one of those times, even though it wasn't related to property.

As Pua stood there in the kitchen her phone rang. She almost never took a call when with a client signing papers, and Sam was the most significant client she'd ever had. But when she saw it was Uncle Jin, she picked up.

"Uncle," she answered.

Jessica reached out toward Pua. "I want to talk to him," she said firmly.

Pua ignored Jessica and turned away from her. "I'm here with Sam and Jessica. I'll tell them." And then she hung up the phone.

Jessica's nostrils flared, and her brow furrowed when Pua didn't hand her the phone.

"He said you'd find what you're looking for on board Uncle's boat at the harbor."

The anger left Jessica just as fast as it had come. "Let's go," she barked, and they piled into Pua's Mercedes and raced to the harbor. To protect Pua, she and Sam never told her what was on the boat, and Pua was smart enough not to ask.

Jin Tanaka's forty-five-foot Hatteras was in its slip, with the key in it, and not a soul around when Pua dropped Sam and Jessica off at the harbor. It had been a long time since Jessica handled such a big yacht, and she decided the smart thing to do was let Sam take the helm, since he had a lot more experience handling big boats than she did. As they walked to the slip, Sam remarked, "Nice boat."

"And who said crime doesn't pay?" Jessica muttered. "It's going straight to the bottom if we don't get Jasmine back. And I might sink it anyway."

"Could you not sink it while I'm on board?" Sam asked in a joking kind of way, as he tried to ease the tension.

"We'll see," Jessica said with a half smile.

Sam started the big Caterpillar engines, Jessica cast off the lines, and they idled out of Honokohau Harbor toward the open sea. Jessica had fished these waters with her father when she was growing up and knew them well enough to point Sam in the right direction toward VV buoy, where the exchange was supposed to take place. The buoy was only about four miles offshore of Kailua Bay.

Woo Ching was supposed to meet them at the rendezvous point in a cigarette boat, it would be easy to spot, since they were a rare boat in Hawaiian waters.

As they approached the buoy, Jessica had binoculars pointed at the horizon, and looked for any fast-approaching boats. Nothing. It was almost six p.m. The dope was in a duffle bag that laid next to the fighting chair at the rear of the boat.

A few minutes later, a thirty-eight-foot Top Gun cigarette

boat approached the Hatteras from the north at a high rate of speed. "That thing must be going over eighty knots. If you planned on chasing them down after getting Jasmine back, that's not happening," Sam said.

"I just want her safely on board. I'll look for Woo Ching later, after we get Jasmine back to Aloha Village," Jessica replied.

Sam and Jessica checked their guns and then re-holstered them with the safeties off, ready to rock–if they had to. Jessica had eyes on Woo Ching through her binoculars and could see Jasmine seated at the back of the boat with her hands bound behind her. Her waist-length, dark brown hair blew in the wind. Jasmine was less than a quarter of a mile away from being freed. A radio call from the Coast Guard came over the VHF marine radio on the Hatteras and jolted Sam and Jessica out of their focus on Jasmine. They hadn't noticed the Coast Guard response boat, that had come upon them from behind out of the south, intent on boarding the Hatteras.

"You've got to be kidding me," Sam said.

"Quick, hide the guns and the dope," Jessica ordered Sam. "I'll stall them." Jessica clicked the safety back on and handed Sam her Glock, she hoped the Coast Guard crew didn't see the handoff with binoculars.

As soon as Woo Ching saw the flashing blue light of the Coast Guard response boat, he hooked a hard U-turn, opened up the throttle on the Top Gun racer and disappeared into the sunset.

It became evident as the Coast Guard boat approached the Hatteras that this would not be an inspection for lifejackets. Four petty officers were stood at the front of the response boat, and held M4 rifles. They were there to look for drugs, and they meant business. Lau had set a trap and Sam and Jessica had walked right into it. He was willing to donate ten kilos of China White if it meant Jessica would be behind bars and out of the way.

Jessica pulled her cell phone out and hit the button to dial Uncle Jack. As usual, he didn't answer. "I don't have time to explain. Jasmine was kidnapped and is on a boat heading north from VV buoy. I'd check the Puako boat ramp for a cigarette boat getting pulled out of the water. That's the guy who has her. The Coast Guard will probably arrest me and Sam in a few minutes, and that's why I'm telling you this. Go find the guy with that boat, and you'll find Jasmine." Then she hung up.

The Coast Guard petty officers boarded the Hatteras and searched it until they found the drugs. Jessica and Sam tried to explain that they were trying to exchange them for Jasmine. The petty officer in charge of the boarding party was empathetic and didn't think they were drug dealers, but it wasn't up to him to let them go. He still had his orders to handcuff them and take them into custody.

By this time, Jessica had nothing to lose and begged the Coast Guard to look for the cigarette boat and Jasmine. Once they verified Jessica was a former LA detective, they took her story seriously and dispatched an HC-130 to look for Jasmine.

"The plan had never been to trade Jasmine for the ten kilos of China White. It had always been about getting me arrested for being in possession of the dope. Lau had correctly gambled that I wouldn't call the cops or FBI and I'd try to make the exchange for Jasmine myself."

"And the gamble had paid off," Sam said.

37

NIGHT AT SEA

Woo Ching took Jasmine northwest toward Kohala, and was about ten miles offshore, when he decided that should be far enough. He had a simple plan. Shoot Jasmine in the head and throw her body over the side.

Jasmine had been a competitive free diver in her late teens and had held her breath as long as five minutes. As soon as Woo Ching brought the boat to a stop and shut off the engines, Jasmine knew it was now or never. She tucked into a ball and brought her arms underneath her feet so she could get her hands in front of her. Thank goodness for the yoga class she had taught the last year at the resort she thought, as she performed the maneuver with little effort. She quickly broke the zip tie using a method her karate teacher had showed her. She pulled it as tight as possible, then raised her hands over her head and slammed them into her belly.

Woo Ching had his back to Jasmine and hadn't paid attention until she stood up with her arms in front of her and snapped the zip tie he had wrapped around her wrists. As Woo Ching turned toward her, he pulled a snub-nosed .357 Magnum out of his pocket. He brought the gun up to fire, but

Jasmine was lightning fast and dove over the back of the boat, into the water before he got a round off in her direction.

She only had seconds to hyperventilate before she went in the water, but it was enough to allow her to get a big gulp of air. She also knew she risked shallow-water blackout if she hyperventilated, but it was her only choice.

Jasmine had a simple idea. She dove deep and held her breath long enough to make Woo Ching think she was dead. But her plan hadn't included him putting a bullet in her.

Woo Ching fired a half a dozen rounds into the water from the back of the boat. She watched them streak past her like torpedoes. All of them narrowly missed her, except one that struck and passed through her left hand. Jasmine didn't realize she had been shot until she saw the blood in the water.

Jasmine's lungs burned for air more than she could ever remember. But she knew if she gave in to the desire for air and surfaced, she was dead. Jasmine struggled to stay submerged, and used the least amount of energy possible. With no weight belt on and her lungs full of air, her body wanted to surface, as she fought to stay down under the boat. It was simple physics.

After close to four minutes, all Woo Ching saw was blood in the water. He thought for sure she was dead. He started up the engines, and headed back to the launch ramp at Puako.

When Jasmine couldn't hold her breath another second, she floated to the surface and prayed Woo Ching wouldn't see her. By then, he was a quarter of a mile away and she was safe–for the time being.

She had cupped her left hand as best she could, to cover the bullet hole and stop the bleeding, as she floated on the surface. She knew if she didn't get the bleeding stopped, sharks would appear soon and end it for her. Jasmine took off her T-shirt, ripped it with her teeth and wrapped a four-inch-wide swath around her hand as a bandage.

She had trained for the annual Hawaii triathlon for the last two years. She could swim three miles, but she had never swum more than that. If she wanted to live, she'd have to swim three times further than she ever had, and with a bullet hole in her hand. She wasn't ready to die yet; the only thing that kept the pain at bay was the fear she would not make it to shore.

It was late in the afternoon, and the ocean surface had light swells about a foot high, with visibility close to a hundred feet down. Jasmine could see shadows in the water below her, and out of the deep, appeared a big shadow about fourteen feet long. Soon it became clear, even without goggles, it was a tiger shark. The blood from her wound had attracted the shark. The upside was the shark didn't act like it was going into a feeding frenzy, as they were known for doing just before they attacked.

The apex predator circled Jasmine for about ten minutes, looked her over as if deciding whether it wanted to have lunch or not. Jasmine was an island girl and had seen sharks before while she swam close to shore. It was no big deal then, because all one had to do was just get out of the water. But this was different. There was nowhere to go. The tiger started to dart back toward Jasmine, and she knew she would die right there as soon as it attacked. Suddenly out of the blue came another shadow from the deep, and then another and another. *"Great, he's called his buddies, and now it's going to be over. At least it'll be fast,"* she said out loud to no one but herself.

But this time it wasn't sharks–it was a pod of dolphins, they surrounded Jasmine and formed a barrier between her and the shark. And the shark, just as quickly, decided to look elsewhere for its lunch.

As Jasmine swam toward the shore, she looked toward Mauna Kea from time to time so she knew she was going the right direction. But the problem was, the mountain didn't get closer–only smaller.

She told herself, *You can do this*. But the current was headed *away* from the island and went toward Japan. Even though she had the stamina to swim ten miles, she couldn't break free of the riptide that carried her away from the island.

The dolphins stayed close to her, they never left her alone, as she floated on her back for a while to rest and think about what to do next.

Exhausted, she thought how easy it would be just to give up and slide beneath the surface of the ocean. And then she thought of the pain it would cause her sisters, besides, she wasn't ready to go just yet. She decided she would try to swim two miles south, to see if she could get out of the current she was in, and then try swimming toward the island.

Jasmine swam south for thirty minutes with everything she had. The island had disappeared from sight and it had started to get dark. She could see the stars become visible in the eastern sky. She rolled over on her back again to enjoy the view one more time before she would die. After an hour, she was almost hypnotized by the beauty of the stars that twinkled in the night sky. By this time, she figured she had drifted a long way from the Big Island and the end was near.

As she thought about how she'd never see her family again she was bumped by a small log that jolted her out of her thoughts. At least it wasn't a shark, she thought, after the initial fear had passed. It was debris from the Japanese tsunami that had made its way into Hawaiian waters. There was a sliver of a moon out, and it provided just enough light that she could see something else bobbing up and down, about three hundred feet away.

It took almost all the energy she had left to swim to the object. It was a dock that had broken free and floated all the way to Hawaii. It had a rope that hung off one of its cleats into the water. She barely had the strength to swim to the dock, much less pull herself up on top of it. After she rested for a while, as she hung on to the rope, she felt she might have the strength to climb.

The pain in her hand was excruciating as she pulled herself. "You can do this," she whispered. She wanted to let go, but she knew if she did, she was as good as dead. By the last pull on the line, she reached up and grabbed the cleat at the edge and pulled herself all the way up on the dock, where she collapsed, and panted, unable to move another inch. She was dehydrated and exhausted, but now she had a chance to live long enough to be found—if she could collect some rainwater before dying of thirst.

AS THE SUN CAME UP, the dolphins reappeared. Not just the ten or twenty that had saved her from the shark the day before, but hundreds of dolphins,–if not a thousand.

Great, I've become the dolphin queen, she thought. Then she yelled, "Does anybody have a boat?" and laughed until she cried.

There wasn't a cloud in the sky. The weather had been hot and dry the last week, and the forecast called for more of the same. Jasmine had no protection from the sun– and no water. As the hours passed and the sun came overhead, she felt her skin burn, and her tongue felt swollen and had turned into leather all at the same time.

Jasmine was the most positive of the three Murphy daughters, but she found it hard to be positive about anything other than–she would die of thirst.

I can't control this right now, she thought. *I might as well meditate.* She cleared her mind and lay on the dock, and became one with it until she could feel the direction of the ocean swells.

Pili Kalea had been the waterman at Aloha Village for many years before he passed, and he had taken all the

Murphy sisters out on the water and shared his knowledge of the sea with them. Pili had taught Jasmine well about the sea. He had shown her you could navigate by the stars, and if the weather was cloudy, you could feel the direction you were going in by the ocean's swells.

Jasmine was nowhere near proficient with ancient Hawaiian navigation skills, but she knew enough to tell she was headed toward Molokai, which was a lot better than going to Japan. Still, she didn't let herself get excited. She knew she was much closer to death than she was to living through this nightmare she found herself in.

She sat up straight as soon as she heard the Coast Guard chopper off in the distance. She prayed it was looking for her, but it was too far away, and there was no way to signal it.

The chopper had been on the scene the maximum amount of time and was low on fuel, as it made the turn for Oahu. As Jasmine watched it disappear over the horizon, she felt sad to her core. She began to cry as she thought it was over–and they would never find her.

She was so focused, as she watched it fly off, that she didn't hear the Coast Guard HC-130 come up behind her from the south. They had flown over the southern search grid and worked their way north, when a crew member had spotted something in the water. It was the hundreds of dolphins, not Jasmine, that caught his eye. And then he noticed something in the middle of the pod, a small rectangular object. At first he thought it was only debris in the water. But when he saw Jasmine, as she jumped up and down and waved her arms, he notified the pilot and marked the GPS coordinates.

The HC-130 crew circled until the chopper could refuel and come back. It was almost dusk when the Eurocopter HH-65 Dolphin returned to the scene.

Coast Guard rescue swimmer, Petty Officer Third Class Ryan Stinnett, was lowered out of the chopper down to the dock with a basket. As Jasmine stood up, she collapsed, but Petty Officer Stinnett caught her with one hand, as he held the basket steady with the other. He cradled her in one arm and gently laid her in the basket, then gave the thumbs-up for the crew chief to raise her up to the chopper, as it hovered overhead.

Aboard the helicopter, and on the way to Honolulu, Jasmine realized two things as she looked into the eyes of the man who saved her. One, she would live. And two, she would marry Petty Officer Stinnett someday.

When the HH-65 Dolphin landed at Barbers Point, Oahu, an ambulance standing by, took Jasmine to Queen's Medical Center.

38

ARRESTED

Sam and Jessica were in custody at the federal detention center on Oahu. When they were each allowed to make a phone call, Sam called his lawyer, and Jessica called Uncle Jack.

"Did the Coast Guard find the cigarette boat and Jasmine?" Jessica asked. "No. But I found the boat in Puako. Woo Ching had abandoned it at the dock. I asked everyone at the boat ramp if anyone had seen who had gotten off the boat, a couple of people saw the boat dock. I showed them Woo Ching's photo and they said it was him; he was the only one on the boat. I called the Coast Guard and told them they needed to look for Jasmine north of VV buoy and south of Lapakahi State Park."

The DEA's Drug Task Force sent Agents Stringer and Jones, from the LA office, to Oahu to interview Sam and Jessica. Both agents were in their mid-forties and were seasoned investigators. Their task force had been trying to stop the flow of fentanyl to the US mainland from China via Hawaii. Since Sam and Jessica had been in possession of ten kilos of fentanyl when the Coast Guard had boarded their boat, the agents thought it reasonable to assume Sam and

Jessica knew who the distributor was. The DEA didn't believe a well-connected billionaire and a former LAPD detective were the drug kingpins of Hawaii. But just the same, the feds wanted to know how it came to be that Sam and Jessica were on a boat that had ten kilos of fentanyl on it.

Lau had done a perfect job of setting up Sam and Jessica. They knew they rolled the dice when they decided to go it alone without calling the FBI or Kona PD.

Agent Jones sat across from Jessica in the interview room.

She had slept little the last couple of days; the black circles around her eyes made her look like she was a drug user and didn't help her credibility.

"Ms. Kealoha, can you tell me why the boat you and Mr. Stewart were on had ten kilos of fentanyl on board?"

Jessica told Agent Jones the story of Jasmine's kidnapping and the ransom call that had asked for the drugs.

Agent Jones then asked, "Why didn't you call the FBI or the Kona PD?"

"The FBI headquarters is a half a dozen islands north of Kona, and I figured by the time they got here, my sister would be dead. And the Kona PD, I have trust issues with."

Agent Jones questioned Jessica for the next couple of hours and then compared notes with Agent Stringer who had interviewed Sam. It was apparent they weren't the distributors that the DEA was looking for, and their stories matched. But there was still the issue of the drugs they had been in possession of.

After the agents received a call from their supervisor, they told Sam and Jessica they were free to go. But the feds had seized Jin Tanaka's yacht, which was just fine with Jessica. She didn't know who Sam's lawyer had called, at the DEA headquarters in Springfield, Virginia, but it was someone near the top who had said to let them go. Just like in Hawaii, it helped to know the right people.

After being released from custody, the first thing Jessica

did was check her voicemail. There was a message from a nurse at the Queen's Medical Center that said they had treated Jasmine and she would be okay. Overcome with emotion, Jessica couldn't hold in all her feelings anymore. To know that Jasmine was alive washed away the negative thoughts, that she had sunk into, over the past twenty-four hours. It renewed her faith that sometimes good things happened despite the overwhelming odds, and that it was time to be grateful and savor the moment.

After she caught a taxi over to the hospital, Jessica stopped in the ladies' room so she could fix her face. She didn't mind Sam seeing her look like death warmed over, but she had this thing about always being strong for her younger sister. She wanted to wash her face and put on some makeup to hide the black circles around her eyes. Besides, she didn't want to scare her little sister by looking like a ghoul.

When Sam and Jessica entered Jasmine's room, it surprised them to find six-foot-two Petty Officer Ryan Stinnett there, as he stood next to Jasmine's bed and held her hand. Jessica went to the other side of the bed and gave Jasmine a long hug and a kiss on the forehead.

"Are you okay, honey?" she asked. Jasmine nodded, tears formed in her eyes, and they hugged again.

Ryan and Sam stood back and let the sisters have their moment together. Then Jasmine introduced Ryan. "This is Petty Officer Ryan Stinnett. He saved my life."

Sam and Jessica shook hands with Jasmine's handsome hero as he remarked with a Southern drawl, "It was a team effort. I was just one of many who helped."

Jessica liked this young man, she had a good feeling about him. He was big as a tree and humble as a monk.

As she rubbed Jasmine's hand that wasn't bandaged, she asked her, "How long are you going to be here?"

"The doctor says two days, and then I can go home."

Jessica nodded and pulled a photo of Woo Ching out of

her pocket and showed it to Jasmine. "Was this the guy who kidnapped you?"

Jasmine didn't recognize him from the photo because Woo Ching had disguised himself as an old man. She shook her head.

"Okay, honey. We have to go back to Kona and find the man who did this to you. We'll be back to pick you up when you get discharged." Jessica hugged Jasmine again, before she and Sam left the hospital.

Sam's jet waited on the ramp at the Honolulu airport to take them back to Kona. As the Gulfstream taxied toward the runway, Sam noticed Jessica deep in thought and asked, "What's bugging you?"

"I would have bet my last dollar it was Woo Ching who kidnapped Jasmine. But she says the guy looked a lot older than him. It doesn't add up."

"What if he was wearing a disguise?" Sam asked.

"Hmm, you might be right. I need to find someone to take this photo of Woo Ching to, who has digital enhancement skills, and knows how to make him look much older. Then show it to Jasmine again."

Sam frowned. "We. We need to find someone."

Jessica put her hand on Sam's thigh. "I'm sorry. I'm so used to being alone. I'll practice that *we* word."

Sam placed his hand over Jessica's. "That's better."

A few minutes later, as the jet climbed over Diamond Head, Jessica looked out the window and remarked, "I will find him. And if he resists, which I hope he does–I will kill him."

39

WOO CHING VS. JESSICA

Jasmine had just awakened when she heard a gentle knock on the hospital room door.

"Come in," she said as she attempted to sit up, forgetting her injured hand. The pain caused her to yelp just as Petty Officer Stinnett walked in.

"What's wrong?" Stinnett asked, as he rushed to her bed.

"Oh, hi–I'm okay, just forgot about this," Jasmine said holding up a seriously bandaged hand. Her cheeks flushed then as she thought suddenly more about her hair than her hand.

"Here, let me help you. Do you want to sit up?"

"Uh, yes–please," Jasmine said, and wondered if her gown was closed where it should be.

The handsome sailor flashed a broad smile, adjusted her pillows and gently took her arm as she scooted herself more upright. He then elevated the head of the bed slightly so she could rest against it.

"So, tell me, Petty Officer Stinnett–did you take special classes in rescuing women?" Jasmine inquired, as she brushed her hair back, straightened her gown and smiled up at him.

"As a matter of fact–I did!" he said, as he laughed.

Jasmine laughed and immediately felt comfortable, in spite of how she may have looked. His laughter was sincere and set her at ease. I think *I like this guy,* she thought.

"I just came by to check on you to give you this," he said, as he handed her a phone. "I thought you might want to call your family. And if you need some company, you can call me too, I took the liberty of programming my number in it." He grinned and continued before she could reply, "I heard you will be staying in Honolulu for a while and your sister asked me if I could keep an eye on you. If that's okay with you, of course."

She liked how considerate he was and the effort he had gone to make sure she had his phone number. Jasmine smiled, "Yes, I think that would be great. And, thank you for the phone–and my life." She could feel her cheeks warming as they flushed. Hopefully, it wasn't noticeable, she thought.

Stinnett couldn't contain his grin.

"Okay then, I gotta get back to the base. But if you need anything–anything–don't hesitate to call me, please." He reached over and touched her hand for a brief second as he smiled.

"I will–I promise. Thank you," she said.

❦

AS SOON AS their plane landed in Kona Jessica called Pua.

"Hey, sis, so how was prison life?" Pua teased when she answered the call.

"Well, not my favorite," Jessica said. She expected to get chewed out, but to her surprise, Pua didn't seem mad anymore.

"Uncle Jack told me the Coast Guard rescued Jasmine, and she's safely tucked away in Honolulu. He also said they hauled you and Sam off to jail," Pua said, with a slight giggle. The thought of Jessica locked up temporarily seemed to give Pua a bit of satisfaction.

"Yeah, I thought you'd find that part amusing," Jessica said, as she smiled.

"Okay, I just wanted to check in with you and give you an update, but you're all caught up already. I have some things to do now in Kona," Jessica said.

"Hey, Jess–watch your back and Sam's, too. Okay?"

"I promise, Pua. And you keep a sharp eye on your surroundings." With that, she turned her attention to Sam. With a determined look in her eyes she said, "Let's go catch a bad guy."

The next thing on Jessica's list was to identify Jasmine's kidnapper. She needed to find someone to use age progression software on Woo Ching's photo. After several calls, and no luck, she called a longtime photographer friend.

"Hi Jimmy, this is Jessie from way back when."

"Hey, Jess, long time no hear. Howzit?" said the very happy voice.

"You haven't changed a bit have you, Mr. Sunshine?"

They both laughed.

"Wow, I haven't been called that since high school!"

"Yeah, a lot of surf has passed since then, huh? I'm in need of some skills you might have. I have a photo that needs to age the guy over a couple of decades. Can you do that right away? And sorry to rush, but I'm working a case here in Kona," Jessica said.

"Wow, you're back in the 808. And being all Hawaii Five 0 here again?"

"Well–not exactly," Jessica hesitated.

"Shoots, okay, okay, none of my business," he said.

"I'm on a photo assignment up north at Pololu Valley, so I can't help right now and it sounds like you need this yesterday. I'll text you a couple websites to check that might do what you want, okay?"

"Mahalo, Jimmie and I promise we'll catch a sunset at Old A's," Jessica said.

"No problem, and that'd be great. We can catch up. Okay, I gotta go, too. I'll text the web addresses now. And don't forget to call Mr. Sunshine," Jimmie said, and they both laughed.

"Okay–aloha."

After she found a site to match her skill level, Jessica was able to produce a series of photos that showed Woo Ching aging from his current age, about thirty-five, up to eighty years old.

She then texted them to Jasmine and got an immediate response. Jasmine texted back one of the pictures and said, *"Oh my God, that's the guy. Please get him, Jess!"*

"This is exactly what I needed. You get better. Love you." Jessica texted back.

She stared at the photo that Jasmine had sent back. "We got him!" She said out loud.

"Now it's my turn to put him in the crosshairs."

WOO CHING HAD STALKED Sam and Jessica since they'd returned to Kona. He had a simple plan: slip into Jessica's bungalow and kill them both. He would wait until just the right moment, when they least expected it–to strike.

As he watched, Sam sent his security team back to *The Ohana* in Kailua Bay.

"It will feel especially satisfying watching your last breaths, Ms. Kealoha," Woo Ching muttered to himself.

Jessica had decided to keep Jasmine on Oahu, stashed away in a vacation rental, until Woo Ching was either in jail or dead. And Jessica didn't care which way it ended.

After they had returned to Aloha Village, she had sensed she was being watched, no doubt it was Woo Ching. It was a feeling she had that wouldn't go away. Sam argued that his security team should hang around until they had dealt with Woo Ching. But Jessica knew if Sam's guys left Aloha Village, Woo Ching would eventually show up and try to kill her. Especially given the intel she had gotten from Uncle Jack. He'd said Woo Ching was a notorious hit man in Hong Kong and had never failed to kill a target. Until now. His reputation was on the line. He had to eliminate Jessica, or he would never work again as a contract killer. And he knew too much to be allowed to live.

JESSICA HAD MADE sure word got around that she and Sam were back at the Village, she had known that the mole would pass that along to Lau. It was about nine p.m. when Sam left the bungalow and walked down to the Marlin House restaurant as if going to get a late dinner. Jessica, wore an innocent-looking sundress, walked with him out to the lanai, gave him a hug and a kiss, and watched him walk down the long driveway toward the restaurant. She went back inside, turned off the lights before she sat on the couch–and waited. She had a Glock, in a leg holster under her dress, to keep her company. Sam stayed away for two hours, and watched Jessica via a security camera feed on his phone. Nothing happened.

They repeated the same routine for another two nights. And again, nothing happened. No sign of Woo Ching.

The next morning, when Sam walked out the front door to get the newspaper, a bullet ripped through his right leg as he reached over to pick it up. Woo Ching ran from behind a hedge of naupaka, a hundred yards away, and forced Sam to hobble back inside the bungalow with a gun in his ribs.

Woo Ching had a silencer on the barrel of his rifle, and Jessica was in the shower, oblivious to what just happened, but Comet growled and barked his head off. Jessica came out of the shower to see what the commotion was about. Comet never barked unless there was a stranger at the house. She didn't want to leave the bathroom with only a towel, so she grabbed her board shorts and a t-shirt that hung on a hook. She slowly opened the bathroom door and looked down the hall toward the living room.

She could see Sam sitting on the couch, his face wrinkled in agony while he held his bloody hand over the bullet hole in his leg, and tried to stop the bleeding. Woo Ching stood in the kitchen across from him, with his rifle leaned against the wall and his pistol pointed at Sam.

Jessica could see the blood as it seeped between his fingers. Comet sat at Sam's feet, and growled toward the kitchen. She knew Woo Ching was in the house and she knew he was waiting for her to walk into the living room. She also knew that as soon as she did, he would kill her and Sam.

"I know you're back there, come on out," Woo Ching yelled.

"Why don't you come back here instead?"

"Okay, right after I kill your boyfriend."

"All right, all right, I'm coming out," Jessica yelled. She slowly walked out into the living room and sat next to Sam on the couch. She glared at Woo Ching for a moment, and then said, "I'm going to give you one chance to surrender. Set the gun down on the counter next to you and put your hands behind your head, interlocking your fingers."

Woo Ching laughed as he brought his pistol to bear and then lowered the weapon, as if he had considered it. Jessica had a slight smile and a look of contentment on her face. She was glad he chose not to surrender.

Uncle Jack was in a bungalow two hundred feet from Jessica's with a sniper rifle, and waited for Woo Ching to show up and make his move. He had been in the bathroom when Sam went out to get the paper, but when he'd heard

Comet start barking, he'd run back into the living room, where he had his Remington. After he'd checked the video feed, he saw that Woo Ching was in the house. He looked through the rifle scope and could see him through the window. He was going to kill Sam and Jessica if Uncle Jack didn't act right that second. He aimed the rifle through his window toward the living room window of Jessica's bungalow, as fast as he could, just as they had planned. But Uncle Jack couldn't get a clear shot, as Jessica sat on the couch, until Woo Ching moved toward her.

Woo Ching took two steps toward Sam and Jessica and raised his pistol again. Uncle Jack exhaled and squeezed the rifle's trigger–Woo Ching dropped like a rock.

When the .300 Win Mag slammed into his chest, it must have ricocheted off a bone; the exit wound made one hell of a mess behind him in the kitchen.

Sam, Jessica, and Uncle Jack had rehearsed numerous scenarios if Woo Ching got in the house. Sam getting shot, while going out to get the paper, wasn't one of them. He reminded them a few times, as they waited for an ambulance to arrive.

EPILOGUE

During the investigation of Mike Murphy's crash, the FBI had questioned Simmy and noticed inconsistencies in her story right from the start. After hours of intense questioning, she'd finally admitted she had put the sugar in the airplane's gas tank.

The U.S. attorney in Honolulu charged her with second-degree murder but reduced it to voluntary manslaughter, in a plea agreement, and Simmy took the deal. The judge sentenced her to five years in prison.

THE SKY WAS blue and clear on the morning of Pua's first birthday party after being pronounced cancer free by her doctor. Jessica had rented a pavilion at the Old Airport Beach Park for the celebration; she and Sam had arrived early to decorate the gazebo and get ready for the party.

They placed ti leaves at each corner of the pavilion, as Sam lit the coals on the custom-built grill he'd trailered to the beach for the occasion. There was a bouncy house for the keiki, and lots of tables and chairs where all the aunties and uncles could sit and talk story. Sam got busy barbecuing huli-huli chicken as the crowd gathered.

Over a hundred people had RSVP'd and every starving real estate agent in town, who knew Pua, showed up for a free meal and a chance to pass out their business cards.

Pua's new boyfriend, Charles, played slack key guitar as guests arrived. He was a local musician she had met while at the doctor's office. They lived one day at a time and enjoyed every minute together.

Jasmine and Petty Officer Ryan Stinnett arrived an hour late from Honolulu. They'd missed their flight because Ryan had been delayed returning from an errand that morning. He'd gone to the Ala Moana shopping mall to pick something up for Jasmine. He said it was a secret and wouldn't tell her what it was until the time was right. And it was important to get it before they left for Kona.

Uncle Jack and Kainoa played in waves on their boogie boards until they'd tired of that. Then they checked the lava tide pools to see what kind of cool creatures lurked thereabouts. Kainoa loved to find clownfish and chase crabs. Since Uncle Jin was in prison, on the fentanyl drug charges, Uncle Jack had decided he would fill that void in Kainoa's life. And he realized that relationship had filled something missing in his. Besides, it gave him something to do instead of drinking beer most days.

As Pua's guests congratulated her on her victory over breast cancer, with hugs and plumeria leis of different colors, a shirtless old Hawaiian man, with weathered skin and a long grey-haired ponytail, sat on the beach in front of the pavilion. He started to rhythmically tap his hand against an ipu drum he had carried with him. The sound of the old man's hand, as it slapped the drum, filled the air, and everyone became quiet. The combination of the heel of his hand and fingertips as they hit the drum, created different sounds. It sounded like oo-te-oo-te-te over and over again.

The rhythmic beat of the drum summoned Pua, Jessica, and Jasmine, as though hypnotized. They stood three abreast on the beach, in front of the crowd of at least a hundred and fifty people, and performed a healing hula. They danced and connected with each other and the people as they watched. It was the healing that their family needed at that place and time. Sam had never seen Jessica dance hula before, and didn't realize how much of an island girl she was, until that very moment.

At the end of the hula, everyone clapped and gave the three sisters many hugs. The old Hawaiian casually got up and wandered off down the beach, toward town, with his ipu drum–and a smile.

After he'd disappeared from sight, Sam asked Jessica, "Did you know him?"

She shook her head. "No." Then she looked over at Pua and Jasmine who sat nearby, and they both shook their heads.

BY FIVE P.M. all the guests had left the party, and everything was packed up. Sam and Jessica sat on the beach, and waited for the sunset. Sam hoped this time to see a green flash. Every time he thought he saw it, Jessica swore there was no such thing. They teased each other about it almost every time they watched a sunset together. And they did that as often as they could.

Uncle Jack grabbed a couple bottles of beer out of the ice chest and sat down by them. As he handed one of the bottles to Sam, he said he had some news.

"I thought you guys would like to know, I just got a call a few minutes ago from a friend in Honolulu that I used to work with. He said the FBI arrested Lau as soon as his plane landed in Honolulu earlier today. He was on his way back to Kona from Hong Kong when F-22's, from Hickam Air force base, intercepted his plane and forced it to land on Oahu. The DEA had evidence he was responsible for a murder, and they passed it on to the FBI. So I don't think you need to worry about him causing you any more trouble."

Uncle Jack took a sip of his beer and looked toward the ocean as two dolphins cruised by. "Go home," he yelled. He looked back at Sam and Jessica. "That was Kiki and Koa. They know the street lights are going to be on soon."

Sam and Jessica looked dumbfounded for a moment. "Only in Hawaii," Jessica muttered, as she shook her head, and they all laughed.

Uncle Jack said he had fresh fish for Kiki and Koa at the *A Hui Hou* and needed to get back to the harbor so he could feed them. The dolphins hunted for their food during the day, but could always get a free meal if they came back to the boat at night. Uncle Jack said his good-byes and left so he could get back to the harbor before the dolphins.

Sam and Jessica watched the sun as it started to set on the horizon.

"What are you going to do now that Lau is in prison and the Village is going to be okay?" Sam asked Jessica. Before she could answer, he said, "I know what you should do. You should move in with me and Mr. Jangles at the Keauhou Bay house."

Jessica lightly rubbed Sam's leg as she contemplated her answer. She smiled and said,

"Someone does need to look after you two. It might as well be me."

"I'll take that as a yes."

Jessica scooted closer to Sam, and leaned her head on his shoulder. They watched the sun disappear, and Sam saw what appeared to be a green flash.

"Did you see it?"

"Nope."

He sighed. "You're never going to admit it, right?"

"That's right," she teased.

The End.

Get the free prequel and new release notifications.

https://readerlinks.com/1/965413

The second book in the Hawaii Thriller series is Death Orchid. Here is the first chapter:

Los Angeles

Detective Jessica Kealoha was meeting Special Agent Gabbie Harris for brunch at an outdoor café in Marina Del Rey next to the harbor. Jessica felt serene whenever she was near the ocean. She and Gabbie tried to meet there at least twice a month to have mimosas and blow off steam from the task force they had been assigned to work together on.

As Jessica made her way to the table on the outdoor patio where Gabbie sat, an ocean breeze blew through her hair. She loved the smell of the salt air because it reminded her of growing up in Hawaii.

It was an overcast sky in early June and the temperature was about eighty degrees that Sunday morning in southern California.

The June gloom from the marine layer was in full effect, and Jessica hated it with a passion because she suffered from depression on most of those gray days. Every June all she wanted to do was sleep through the overcast days until July and the return of blue skies.

The café was busy. The owner, Steve, was late-forties and always had a large table reserved on Sundays for an assortment of young women he was trying to sleep with. It was always full of the "beautiful people," as Gabbie liked to refer to them, mostly wannabe actresses with boob jobs and mini skirts that looked like someone had spray painted them on.

By contrast, Jessica wore jeans and a white t-shirt with tennis shoes. She had a subcompact 9mm in a belly band holster hidden under her t-shirt. Gabbie was going to work out afterward; she wore gym shorts and a tank top. Her 9mm was in her fanny pack.

Jessica had noticed Steve liked to chase women in their twenties and never hit on her or Gabbie since they were in their thirties. And they carried guns for a living.

A big crowd was there that day, and Jessica had to squeeze between two packed tables to get to where Gabbie sat. She was glad the diet of the week was finally starting to pay off, since there was a time when her hips might not have glided so easily between the close-together tables.

Jessica and Gabbie had been working together for a year now and had become close friends because they had similar interests outside of work. They talked about everything, not just work.

Gabbie was always trying to fix Jessica up with one of her husband's political colleagues, but Jessica only liked to date other cops.

Gabbie was taking a healthy gulp of her drink when Jessica sat down. Her eyes were puffy. It was obvious she had been crying.

Jessica's eyebrows furrowed when she saw Gabbie's face. "What happened?"

"Karl thinks I'm cheating on him with my trainer at the gym."

Jessica reached over and touched the side of Gabbie's face where it was obvious she had covered a bruise with makeup.

Gabbie looked down toward her drink sitting on the table, and tears began to run down her cheeks.

Jessica reached for Gabbie's hand. "Look at me. I know you guys have been together since high school. But you have to leave him."

"I can't. I'm pregnant."

Jessica's eyes looked straight at the glass in front of Gabbie.

"It's only orange juice."

Jessica nodded.

❧

Two weeks later

Once again Gabbie had lied to the doctor about how she had broken her ribs. Karl made sure not to leave a mark on her face again. He was an expert at how to beat her up and not leave any signs of abuse. An abused wife with a black eye would be career ending for a Senator who campaigned on family values. Unseen injuries didn't require explanation.

But this time Senator Karl Harris had beaten Gabbie one too many times. Over and over through the years he'd sworn he'd never touch her again. This time she would hold him to it for sure. She instinctively knew the only way he would not beat her again was if he were dead. The trick would be to make it look like an accident.

Gabbie knew driving home from the hospital was the perfect time to ask Karl for something he would normally decline. His pattern after beating her had been to take her on a trip afterwards to make up and wash away his guilt. But this time it would be Gabbie who suggested the trip.

As she shifted in the car's seat trying to find a comfortable position, her broken ribs caused a sharp pain every time the car hit a bump in the road. She mustered as much sincerity as she could and said, "Honey, obviously you've been under a lot of pressure lately. Why don't we go to the Grand Canyon for a short vacation? We can take the train from Williams and spend two nights at the lodge at the South Rim of the canyon," Gabbie suggested.

"I don't know, Gabbie. I have a lot of work to do gearing up for my re-election campaign."

Karl paused for a minute and then said with a tone of voice as if he was doing her a favor:

"I suppose I could bring my laptop and do some work from the lodge." Gabbie nodded and turned her head to look at Karl. She smiled, thinking to herself that she'd had enough.

A Week Later

Jessica and Gabbie had cleared a big case that put a lot of Russian mobsters in prison and they were celebrating over dinner and drinks at a local brew pub.

"Karl and I are going by train to the Grand Canyon for a few days. He said he's going to be working on his computer most of the time and I don't want to be there by myself. Why don't you come along and we could see the sights together?" Gabbie said, while she was stirring her soup.

Jessica played with her salad before answering.

"I don't know, I don't want to be a third wheel."

"No, it will be fine, he'll just work all the time and I'll be alone if you don't come."

Jessica nodded. "Okay, if you're sure he won't have a fit, I'll tag along. I've always wanted to ride a train."

"You've never been on a train?"

"What can I say, I grew up on an island."

KARL AND JESSICA traded dirty looks, while waiting at LAX to board their plane for the short flight to Phoenix. Jessica could tell Karl wasn't happy she came along, but she didn't care what he thought since Gabbie was her friend and needed her.

Jessica had never been to the Grand Canyon before, and she was excited to get out and see the sights. She hardly slept the night before, and was awake at 5 a.m.; ready to go but it was still too dark outside. As soon as the morning light began to creep through the windows into her room, she was out the door and walking toward the rim of the canyon. She wanted to be alone the first time she saw the canyon, so she could enjoy the experience without interruption. Then later she would join Gabbie for whatever she wanted to do while Karl stayed in the lodge and worked on his campaign.

There was a small forest between the lodge and the rim of the canyon; the trees were thick and didn't let much light through. It was still so dark Jessica almost walked straight into a large elk grazing on the path a hundred yards from the lodge. She stopped in her tracks and waited for the enormous beast to move off of the trail so she could pass. She decided she didn't want to be at the whim of an unpredictable seven-hundred-pound animal, and doubled back to the lodge so she could take the long way around to the canyon.

Gabbie and Karl were coming out of their room and saw Jessica heading back in their direction.

"There's a big elk on the path. You might want to take the long way with me," Jessica said.

"We'll just have another cup of coffee and wait for it to pass." Karl said with a hint of annoyance.

"Okay, I'm off to find better coffee than what's in my room. We can meet up later."

Gabbie nodded and followed Karl back into their room.

Jessica headed off the long way to the coffee shop near the rim of the canyon.

An hour later she was walking along the rim heading back toward her room at the lodge, when she saw Karl and Gabbie about a hundred yards away. They were strolling toward a rock ledge that jutted out over the edge of the canyon. Jessica thought she would join them and started walking in their direction.

She was about fifty yards away when she saw Gabbie quickly step toward Karl just before he went over the edge. There was a large rock obstructing her view as she got closer to them. What wasn't clear to her was whether Karl had lost his balance and fell, or had been pushed. Gabbie had sat down at the edge of the ledge and watched the sun continue to rise and paint the walls of the canyon in orange and yellow hues. The canyon floor was a thousand feet below and showed Karl no mercy on that early autumn day.

When Jessica walked up, Gabbie sat there with tears streaming down her cheeks. Jessica sat down next to her and as she put her arm around Gabbie, her friend winced. Gabbie opened her jacket and lifted her shirt so Jessica could see the large bruises on her ribcage.

Jessica stared at the yellow and purple bruises and quietly asked, "How many times did he do this to you?"

"One too many. I lost the baby."

They sat there and continued to watch the sun rise and feel the warmth it provided from the early morning chill.

JESSICA CALLED 911 and the park rangers arrived at the scene within a few minutes.

"It was a horrible accident," Gabbie told the ranger who was taking her statement as she sobbed. He took notes as he listened to Gabbie describe the accident. "Karl took a step, slipped and lost his balance, then fell over the edge," she continued.

A separate ranger interviewed Jessica.

"I was fifty yards away and didn't see it happen. I got a text and looked down to see who it was from, when I heard Gabbie scream; I looked up and Karl was gone."

The park rangers called for a helicopter to retrieve Karl's body and told Gabbie, as gracefully as possible, it was going to cost her thirty-five hundred dollars to do so.

People slipped and fell in the canyon all the time. It happened so much there was even a book about all the deaths in the park that had happened that way.

It was an open and shut case as far as the rangers were concerned, and that was the end of it.

At Karl's funeral many fellow politicians testified to what a great loss his death was to the country. Jessica sat next to Gabbie and held her arm, careful not to brush against her broken ribs. They never spoke about it again but Jessica couldn't shake the thought Gabbie had pushed Karl to his death.

Click here to order book two **Death Orchid** and continue reading.

AUTHOR NOTES

Aloha! And mahalo for spending your time and money on this book. I hope you enjoyed it. **If you could please post a review** on Amazon I would be very grateful. Your review is critical to my success as an author and will help me write better books in the future. Mahalo! Click here to post review.

P.S.

If the link doesn't work, sometimes Amazon is finicky, please just type in JE Trent Death in Paradise in the Amazon search box and my book should come right up in the listings.

Thanks again,

J.E. Trent Author

ABOUT THE AUTHOR

J.E. Trent

J.E. Trent is an emerging author of Hawaii crime thrillers.

The Death in Hawaii Series takes place on the Kona side of the Big Island of Hawaii.

J.E. Trent lived in Hawaii over twenty two years and loves sharing his knowledge of the tropical paradise in his novels.

AFTERWORD

At the time when I got the idea for Sam and Jessica, I had been an auto mechanic for about thirty-five years. I was over fifty and my body was screaming at me every morning that I'd better find another way to make a living. Around that time I had written some flash fiction, that I had gotten a lot of positive feedback on. And I thought with some study, that maybe I could write a novel.

After a lot of brainstorming, Sam and Jessica came to be. A billionaire superyacht builder and a retired LA detective. They aren't perfect; they're growing through problems in their lives that people can relate to. They have character defects just like everybody does. But it's how they strive to overcome them and do the right thing, is what I hope to convey in their stories.

During the twenty-two years I lived on the Big Island, I witnessed some amazing things. Those events are where a lot of the inspiration I get comes from. My goal is to intersperse those moments in my writing, creating something unique that you can only get when you read my books.

Hawaii is a magical place. My words will never do it

justice. I hope that readers take away a bit of aloha after spending time with Sam and Jessica.

Mahalo for your support.

J.E. Trent

Hawi
Honokaa
Waimea
Mauna Kea
Hilo
Kona
Hawaii
Pahoa
Mountain View
Captain Cook
Mauna Loa
Pahala
Naalehu

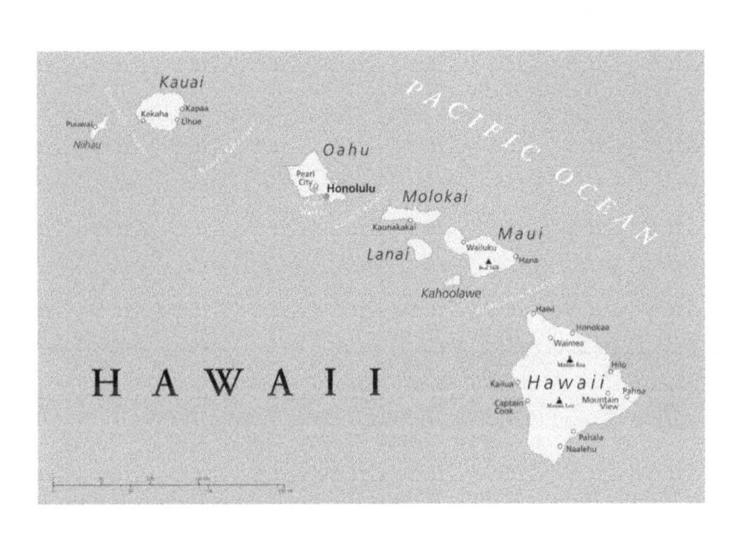
Kauai
Kekaha
Kapaa
Lihue
Puuwai
Niihau
Oahu
Pearl City
Honolulu
Molokai
Kaunakakai
Lanai
Maui
Wailuku
Hana
Kahoolawe
PACIFIC OCEAN
Hawi
Honokaa
Waimea
Hilo
Kailua
Hawaii
Pahoa
Captain Cook
Mountain View
Pahala
Naalehu
H A W A I I

ACKNOWLEDGMENTS

My wife, Eila Trent for editing and her suggestions that have led to Death in Paradise being the best book that it is today.

Shane Rutherford at Dark Moon Graphics made the beautiful cover for the book.

Mahalo to all the authors who have shared their knowledge at kboards.com and the 20BooksTo50K Facebook group and many others.

HAWAIIAN GLOSSARY

Mana (Ma-Na)

Spirit

Aina (Eye-Na)

Land of the island.

Honu (Ho-Nu)

It is a green sea turtle.

Malama (Ma-La-ma)

To take care of.

Hapa (Ha-Pa)

Means mixed race. Hawaiian, Chinese, Japanese, Portuguese and Filipino make up the majority of the population in Hawaii and when they marry their children are called hapa. A mixture.

Huli-huli chicken is grilled on a trailer in a parking lot or on the side of the road. It's usually related to a fundraiser.

Da-Kine (dah-KINE) is a fill-in word used for anything you can't remember the name of.

Aloha (ah-LOH-hah)

Aloha is "hello" and "goodbye." You could also have the spirit of aloha = Giving, caring.

Mahalo (mah-HA-loh)

Means "thank you."

Haole (HOW-leh)

It's used to refer to white people. It can be used offensively, but isn't always meant to be insulting. Originally it meant foreigner, but I seriously doubt anyone uses it for that anymore.

Kane (KAH-neh)

Kane refers to men or boys.

Wahine (wah-HEE-neh)

Wahine refers to women or girls.

Keiki (KAY-kee)

This word means "child." You may hear locals call their children "keiki."

Hale (HAH-leh)

Hale translates to "home" or "house." It can often refer to housing in general.

Pau (POW)

When you put the soy sauce bottle down, you may hear a local ask, "Are you pau with that?" Pau essentially means "finished" or "done."

Howzit (HOW-zit)

In Hawaii, "howzit" is a common pidgin greeting that translates to "hello" or "how are you?"

Lolo (loh-loh)

When someone calls you "lolo," they're saying you're "crazy or dumb." It's sometimes used in a teasing manner.

Ono (OH-noh)

Ono means "delicious." It can often be paired with the pidgin word "grinds," which translates to "food." So, if you eat something delicious, you might say it's ono grinds.

Ohana (oh-HAH-nah)

Means family.

Tita (tit-uh)

Refers to a woman or teenage girl who could be said to either be a tomboy or else somewhat aggressive, tough, or rough with her language or manners.

BOATING GLOSSARY

Saloon = Living room. The social area of a larger boat is called the *saloon*. However, it is pronounced "salon."

Cockpit = Is a name for the location of controls of a vessel; while traditionally an open well in the deck of a boat outside any deckhouse or cabin, in modern boats they may refer to an enclosed area.

Head = Is the bathroom.

Galley = Kitchen.

Stateroom = Bedroom.

Line = Rope.

Port = Standing at the rear of a boat and looking forward, "port" refers to the entire left side of the boat.

Starboard = Standing at the rear of a boat and looking forward, "starboard" refers to the entire right side of the boat.

This book is a work of fiction created between the ears of J.E. Trent.

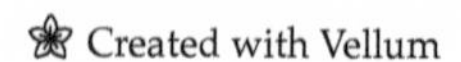

Lightning Source UK Ltd.
Milton Keynes UK
UKHW010635200521
384056UK00001B/150